The Girl in the Scarlet Chair

Haunting Clarisse—Book 1

JANICE TREMAYNE

Janice Tremayne

2nd Edition
Copyright © 2019, 2020 Janice Tremayne
www.janicetremayne.com
author@janicetremayne.com

First published in Australia in 2019

Cover illustration and design by Momir Borocki
(www.99designs.com.au)
Pro/99designs

Edited by AJC Publishing—Australia

Published by Millport Press

Printed and bound by IngramSpark

Digital ISBN: 978-0-646-80634-1
Paperback ISBN: 9798644675449

DEDICATION

For my children, Anthea, Christian, Ernest and Matteo.

Janice Tremayne

CONTENTS

Janice Tremayne

ACKNOWLEDGMENTS

Writing a novel about ghosts, supernatural and the paranormal is one of the most significant projects I have ever committed to completing. It was different from the genre I had written in before (which was job hunting and self-help business blogs), and it presented many challenges.

I want to acknowledge my partner, for their patience and tolerance for the many hours I spent in coffee shops writing my first draft.

I want to thank my book-cover designer, Momir Borocki, for designing a stunning visual cover, and my editor, AJ Collins, for polishing up my work.

Although I am the author of this book, I am not a singular entity. I recognise that it was the kindness of the people around me that motivated me to complete it. I want to thank God for the gift and pleasure of writing. Nobody knows why we become writers. It's a passion drawn from our inner self and a desire to tell beautiful stories that keep us going.

Janice Tremayne

1 THE CHAIR OF DESIRE

Clarisse Garcia was sitting in the garden on an old wooden bench at the back of her mother's house where she had grown up. She was sipping iced tea—it was a humid day and typical for this time of year. She was enjoying the scent of the white flowers coming into bloom. Her mother, Marlita, lived in a town two hours' drive from the sprawling city of Manila. Now she enjoyed spending her days off work there; it was her favourite place to reflect and calm down. The garden and the scent brought back a moment from her childhood when she was questioning her mother about something that she didn't know back then would change her life.

"Mother, why is this room always locked?"

"It's not a room for little girls, my dear. Best not go

inside."

"What's in the room?" Clarisse asked.

"Just an old scarlet chair and a family altar … to remember your great-grandmother, Elena."

"What about the smell that comes from the room?"

"Oh, that's nothing … just rotting flowers."

"But the smell is there for days …" She was an inquisitive little girl.

"It's OK, I will clean the room today," Marlita said.

"What about the noise, Mother? Is there someone in there?"

"There is no one in there, my dear … it's the birds playing on the tin roof—nothing to worry about."

Marlita looked Clarisse in the eye, holding her shoulders firmly, and said, "Promise me you will never go in that room … promise me!"

Clarisse had just heard that her fiancé of five years was playing around. He was seen at a bar not far from his place of work with the same girl on more than one occasion. The source of her information was reliable because they worked in the same company. Her partner made a habit of going missing every Monday night without fail. It was his work commitments, a catch-up day for essential deadlines on a project, that kept him away until late—that is what he made her believe until she wised up.

Clarisse was no stranger to his infidelity; it had happened before. But he was always able to come up with an alibi, accusing her that she was paranoid—too possessive and demanding. She was unlucky in love and desperate to keep her man and maintain the perfect relationship. But was having an ideal relationship expecting too much from her fiancé?

"The majority of relationships are not one hundred per cent perfect, and they have their tribulations," a good friend once told her.

But Clarisse was not buying into this argument because she expected loyalty and trust. She gave all her heart and dedication to him, trying hard to make it work, expecting the same in return.

Angry in the heat of the moment, she decided to take a stand and not in the typical sense—it was more mysterious. She had a plan to break the rules that her family had lived by for one hundred years. Her friends described it as superstition that had grown out of proportion, become exaggerated over time—a frightening tale of consequences that started with her great-grandmother, Elena Enrique, one hundred and fifty years ago. Her mother, Marlita Garcia, was born believing this superstition and nurtured it while she was growing up.

Many people described Clarisse as the embodiment of Elena. If there was any truth in the theory that genes can skip one or two generations, then one had to look no further than Clarisse. Elena was a beautiful woman with striking looks that drove men to extreme lengths to court her. She could have any man in the town, and they even came from neighbouring areas to try their luck. Back in her days, courting a woman required showering them with gifts and serenading them. Marlita often recalled tales of men singing outside Elena's house with a trio of guitar players that went well into the night. Elena was always immaculately well-presented and modelled the best clothes. Her black hair was perfectly tied back into a bun and accentuated with a white flower—like a Spanish dancer. She had brilliant white teeth and an infectious smile that lit up her face; you could see it from a mile away. When she walked down the street, an aura surrounded her, and people noticed her presence. Despite all her beauty, she was a humble and kind person—always helping others in need. The townspeople loved her more for her values and her care for others, rather than her looks.

Clarisse recalled growing up in a home that was loving,

caring and full of warmth. Her mother was pedantic and always fussed over her every need. Being an only child meant she got all the attention she needed and the best of everything. There was nothing too much for Marlita when it came to making Clarisse happy. However, her mother would stop short of spoiling her altogether, and an imaginary line existed between having and having too much. Clarisse had to do her regular household chores and help out wherever she could. But living under the shadow of the family superstition had its challenges. Everyone in the street knew about it and so did her friends at school. Some took it seriously while others baulked at it. Every family in the Philippines had a superstition, or more than one—it was their culture to lay claim to something spiritual and mysterious.

As a child, she was not allowed to enter the room with the scarlet chair or meddle with the altar dedicated to their dead relatives. That was left for once a year, on the Day of the Dead, when they paid homage to those that had passed on to another life. Her mother had warned her not to sit in the scarlet chair and that a dark spirit circled it day and night, ready to capture your soul and whisk you away to a horrible, dark place. As a ten-year-old child, it was a scary and chilling rendition of a superstition that carried on to her late teens.

No one understood the power of the scarlet chair, other than it was shrouded in an old story that Marlita clung onto in memory of Elena's tale. Was it a negative, unhappy chair that had embodied the energy in retribution for an unforgivable act a century ago? An object cannot hold the spirit of someone who has passed away, even though they may not have moved on to the other side. However, an object can keep the energy of that person for a long time—if that energy can be fed and nurtured with superstition carried by generations. The power can be positive, negative or in between, or evolve into something more sinister. Marlita never explained how bad the energy was, only that it had a negative side and was best left alone. She never wanted anyone to interfere with the scarlet chair for fear of raising its awareness or consciousness.

Clarisse became rebellious when she was sixteen years of age. It all happened very quickly, and she went from being a considerate, gentle and obedient girl to one that questioned everything. Marlita was philosophical and believed she was becoming aware of her environment. Her stubbornness led to a situation that her mother would regret later. Clarisse used the energy of the chair to obtain a premonition when she was a teenager, and it nearly destroyed her life. It happened during a time of immense love and heartache, and the chair was her only escape. Clarisse understood it was dangerous and Marlita always made sure she was aware of its sinister side. A chair that could foretell future relationships may sound like a fanciful idea to some, but in her family, it was a well-known secret.

The scarlet chair was a chesterfield and an impressive design—perfect stitching and immaculate leather that had stood the test of time. It was pristine, polished and in excellent condition, considering its age. It was situated in the middle of a dark, timber-panelled room at the back of the house. At the end of the chair was a rendered brick wall that was hastily built. There were no windows and only picture frames on the console table of her grandmother, grandfather, Elena and close relatives. Next to the console table was a small, round table large enough to support a wooden cross, a tribute to Saint Michael the Great. The room was also a shrine to the dead with an altar where Marlita would often pray to the departed loved ones.

The dark room was never meant to be the main attraction, or accessible to guests. It was tucked away for privacy—a place of prayer. Marlita always kept the room meticulously clean and made sure the chair was free from dust. She liked to pick flowers from her garden, and a white flower known as the jasmine sambac by locals. The strong jasmine fragrance it produced penetrated into the hallway outside the room, such was the strength of its scent.

It was an odd place to have such a beautiful chair, and even more peculiar that it was the only piece of furniture in the room besides the console table. Was it a monument to the dead, or did it carry some other religious significance? The chair was lonely, in the dark, and it must have been angry. However, the room was never intended to be a dark place of mystery; it evolved that way over a long time as the superstition took hold. Nobody sat on the chair out of fear they would suffer its wrath. Clarisse's mother always reminded her it was out of bounds, and she reinforced it as Clarisse got older. She was led to believe that sitting in the chair would bring dire consequences and unleash negative energy with evil connotations.

Clarisse understood the dark energy in the chair had the power to access your desire and foresee the outcome of any relationship. It could feel your mental anguish and pain—your feelings, frustration, anxiety and intensity— and take hold of it for pleasure. But it could also torment you if you sat on it for the wrong reasons.

Clarisse had had enough of her partner's infidelity, and

it was messing with her head. She was desperate to find out the truth, and this was her only way—to seek a premonition from the chair. No private detectives to spy on her fiancé, no confessions and no assumptions—just the chair of desire.

Clarisse planned to sit on the chair and take it as it came, such was the desperation to find out about her fiancé's infidelity. She peeked into her mother's room to see if she was asleep and then tiptoed her way to the back of the house. Marlita was sensitive to noise, and a light sleeper, which meant that she had to be extra careful not to prompt her. The sound of clatter in the kitchen or a squeaky door was enough to wake her.

The room with the scarlet chair was locked, and Clarisse went back to find the key in the kitchen. Although Marlita would hide the key in different places to confuse her, she was predictable, and it could only be in one of three locations. She found the key under the sugar jar in the pantry and silently made her way back to the dark room. She put the key in the lock and jiggled it a few times. The lock was the same one Elena used— it's remarkable that it still worked due to its age. After a few twists, she managed to open the squeaky door halfway. A gush of humid air washed over her body, causing her skin to manifest goose bumps all over her arms and legs—and a slight chill came over her body which gave rise to an instantaneous shiver. The change in room temperature was surreal, considering it was a typical warm and humid night.

She briskly walked over to the Edwardian lampshade—the only source of light in the room—and turned it on with an old-style chord that required her to tug it once. The light accentuated the scarlet colour of the chair as she stood gazing at its presence in the middle of the room. She could feel it waiting for her, and it was thirsty for her tales of lust and desire. The negative energy radiating from the chair absorbed her, begging for her to come forward and share her pain. It preyed on bad relationships, adultery and infidelity between lovers. However, it could not deny true love and was powerless without your conceptions of lust and desire. The chair had to be used in the right way and not for retribution, or it would drain your mind and leave you in an exhausted state.

She removed her slippers and walked barefoot to the chair—hesitantly at first but not frightened. She caressed the deep grain of the smooth leather in circular motions until she built up the strength to take a seat—moving slowly and adjusting herself until she was sitting upright with both hands firmly placed on the armrests. Clarisse was staring at the door, waiting anxiously, because she knew what came next. The chair would connect with her inner self and link into her pain and desire. Her pulse was pumping and racing, and she could feel the thumping of her heartbeat. A chill shook her body, and her hands were cold as ice. Her ears developed a tingling sensation, and the luscious soft curls in her hair became straight.

Although it was a warm night, she was shivering, and her clothing offered no relief. Her slender legs started to tremble at the knees. Clarisse wanted to go back to her room, but it was too late for that—the power of the chair captured her.

Apparitions of her partner drinking and flirting with a younger woman raced across her mind. They were holding hands, caressing and kissing voluptuously in a hotel room. She recognised the hotel, and it had a sleazy reputation for short stays—the type frequented by couples looking for a cheap place to have a two-hour fling.

Clarisse didn't like it, but it's what she had come to see. The chair was taking satisfaction from her pain and increased the intensity of the revelation. Then, another hotel room used by couples was projected in front of her. It was the hotel near her fiancé's workplace on the east side of Manila—and there he was with a different woman. They were naked in a bed of sin, coupling. Now she understood the truth—but at what expense to her frailty? Her fiancé's infidelity was more significant than she anticipated. It wasn't just one woman, but a parade of them at his beck and call.

The chair was not done with her yet, and the room started spinning while the lamp flickered on and off consistently in a rhythmic sequence. She was dizzy and disorientated, holding her head with both hands. The room spun faster, and the light became more intense. Green, blue, red and yellow—flicker, flicker, flicker. The chair started vibrating side to side. She tried desperately to get off the chair, but something was holding her down and pushing on her chest.

"Let me go … let me go!" she yelled profusely. "I'm done with you!"

Clarisse wanted to scream and scream again—and disconnect herself from the uncanny thoughts of the chair. But the chair would have none of it, and like many times before, it held her captive. The outline of an older woman's hand with a gold ring on the index finger appeared from the armrest in a curling motion. It pushed onto her torso and held her down from the stomach with force. It was a cold hand, uncomfortable and with a granular feel. An image of Elena as a young woman flickered across her mind—pointing at her and shaking her head with disappointment. Elena was trying to convey a warning about her relationship. It was a sign of her pending separation from her fiancé, and it was being foretold.

It was all too much for Clarisse, and she fainted, collapsing onto the wooden floorboards, bumping her head on an elegantly carved leg. The chair's thirst excruciated her memories in return for the truth, and it rendered her helpless. Clarisse suffered its wrath once more, and her search for love and truth had taken its toll on her. She needed help but could not scream. She wanted to run but could not move. The negative energy of the chair was holding her back and would not let go.

The next morning, Marlita was frantically looking for her daughter.

"Clarisse, Clarisse … are you there?" she said, scouring the house room by room until worry gripped her. There was only one room left to check, and it belonged to the scarlet chair. She dropped her coffee on the floor, trembling, and dashed to the backroom to find her sprawled on the floor next to the chair. She had a cut on her head and was bleeding.

"Oh my God, what has happened to you, my child?" She put her ear to Clarisse's mouth and could hear her breathing.

"Wake up, wake up," she said, patting her gently on her face. There was a groan from Clarisse as she responded to her mother's attempts to revive her. She was alive and regaining consciousness, although very slowly. She looked sleepy and could barely open her eyes; she was dazed and bewildered—she fell in and out of consciousness intermittingly. She was fearless and brave but also a risk-taker. Her mother would have never advised her to sit in the chair to extract the truth—she knew what it was capable of, and the ramifications were not worth it.

Marlita was not a big woman, she was physically unable of carrying Clarisse to her bedroom. She had her mobile phone with her all the time and called her brother-in-law next door for help.

"Clarisse, what have you done? I have told you never to use the chair this way … it's forbidden." Marlita held her tightly in her arms while gently caressing her forehead. "Now we have to go through this all over again in the name of love." She was angry with Clarisse but even more so with the chair. She stared at it with stark intensity, pointing to it fervently.

"Look at what you have become, Grandmother," she said to the chair. "Even with your own flesh and blood, you cannot curtail yourself!"

Marlita was aware Clarisse's fiancé had been unfaithful more than once but never addressed it with Clarisse, opting to stay out of the relationship instead. There was a level of guilt she had to endure as a mother. If she had been closer to Clarisse, she could have found a way to express her broken heart. At the same time, she also understood that Clarisse was stubborn and kept things to herself. She had had the same characteristics when she was a child and had never changed. Considering Clarisse's personality, having a deep and meaningful discussion was always going to be challenging.

Clarisse was groggy and not making sense, mumbling words while gesturing with her hands. Her uncle Pablo came rushing into the room, fearful of what to expect.

"Did you bring the pellegrina with you?" Marlita asked.

"Yes, I have it here." Her uncle Pablo unfolded it from the pouch and placed it over Clarisse.

"This will help bring her spirit back and ward off the negative energy," Uncle Pablo said.

The pellegrina is a short shoulder cape reaching to the elbow only worn by cardinals in the Catholic church. The scarlet chair rattled at the sight of the pellegrina. The two forces of negative and positive energy collided with one another. Uncle Pablo only used the pellegrina as a last resort. Otherwise, it remained in the sacred pouch, tucked away in his altar drawer.

As soon as Uncle Pablo placed the pellegrina around Clarisse's shoulders, the shivering stopped immediately, and her bright red cheeks returned to normal colour. How her uncle Pablo managed to get hold of such a sacred object was unbeknown to everyone. He never discussed it openly with family.

Uncle Pablo lifted and carried Clarisse to the car, gently resting her slender frame into the back seat. He was ready to take her to the hospital—where she spent two months the last time this happened. There was no way of telling how long her recovery could take as there was no science to support an assessment of this phenomenon. But how do you explain to a doctor that it was the result of superstition—who would believe it was because of a scarlet chair? Marlita had been through this before and knew the drill: keep your mouth shut and hope for a speedy recovery.

The superstition endured and became entrenched in her family culture in the following one hundred years. In her native tongue, it was referred to as *pamahiin*. It was the making of a broken heart and enduring love that originated with Elena and ended in a tragedy. They never talked about how Elena died and the drama that followed. It was a guarded secret and for a good reason—only Marlita knew the circumstances that led to her tragic end.

"Clarisse, my dear … we are taking you to the hospital now … can you hear me?" Marlita said while holding back her tears. "There is no need to worry—I will be with you the whole time."

Clarisse nodded in acknowledgment but could not speak a word.

With the help of Uncle Pablo they adjusted the seatbelt and made sure it was firm enough to stop her from bumping herself on the frame of the car. They were ready to take her to the hospital—the same one when a similar episode occurred.

Clarisse's fiancé was nowhere, he had gone missing during the evening with his mistress. He did not return home that night and was unaware of what had happened. He was not answering Clarisse's messages as she desperately tried to contact him the previous night. Marlita blamed Clarisse's fiancé for what happened and considered him the source of the problem. She was in no mood to call him and inform him Clarisse was in the hospital. As far as she was concerned, he was scum and not a good fit for her daughter. The sooner she got rid of him, the better for everyone.

Upon arriving at the hospital, Marlita explained to the doctor on duty that Clarisse had had an anxiety attack and blamed it on her fiancé. It was a credible story that would get her admitted without too many questions. Clarisse was vague and mentally drained. She could not recall what happened and had trouble understanding where she was as disorientation set in. She could not recognise the people in the room except for her mother. She mumbled words that did not make sense and lacked clarity in her vocabulary. The symptoms were the same as when she was admitted as a teenager.

Marlita had been through this before and knew what to expect. It would be a minimum of two weeks of recovery before Clarisse could be her usual self again.

For one straight week Marlita and Uncle Pablo spent every day and evening at the hospital by her bedside. They were taking turns looking after her every need to ensure she could make a speedy recovery. Clarisse was making good progress in hospital and was able to communicate. She was on the path to recovery and confident she would return home soon. Marlita and Uncle Pablo continued visiting every day to make sure she had family around her.

Her uncle Pablo was a kind and considerate man, always there to help the family. He never asked for anything in return or expected favours from others. For him, it was God's work, and he remained a deeply religious man. Uncle Pablo grew up with the superstition of the scarlet chair as a young boy and understood its powers. Now in his late fifties and getting older, the notion was starting to wear him down. He did not have the same energy as before, and every struggle with the chair became harder each time. Nevertheless, even though he walked with a stooping back and a slight limp in his right leg, he always found the strength to support his family.

"Mother, I still can't remember what happened," Clarisse said.

"It was an accident, my dear … all the stress caused by your fiancé and the worries caught up with you."

"That's what the doctor has been saying also. But I remember going into the room with the scarlet chair, and then everything went blank."

"Are they flashbacks or memories?" Marlita asked.

"No, they usually happen in my dreams, and then I wake up suddenly—sweating all over. Sometimes I am so wet I need to shower and change again." Clarisse was almost in tears but managed to hold herself together.

"I'm sure that has to do with the trauma of what you've been through." Marlita took her hand and gently caressed it. "On a positive note, the doctors have told me you have made significant progress in the last couple of days, and if it continues, you will be going home soon."

"Mother, I can't wait to go home again. But there is a problem ..." Clarisse stalled for a moment and looked at her.

"Yes, I know, my dear. He has to leave the house before you return," Marlita said.

"Mother, I don't want him in my sight ever again." Clarisse was feeling emotional and shed a tear.

"Don't worry. Your uncle Pablo and I will deal with it." Marlita brought a photo of Clarisse's fiancé to make a point. She took it out of her bag and tore it to shreds in front of her. "I will make sure you never have to be with that unfaithful bastard ever again."

Marlita gave her daughter a big hug, caressing her hair with her fingers and gently patting her on the back. However, she realised she had a problem on her hands. She had already told Clarisse's fiancé to leave the house many times and he had refused, demanding to see Clarisse to make amends.

Clarisse's fiancé was having a difficult time coming to terms with the thought that his time was up, and Clarisse wanted nothing to do with him. How was Marlita going to resolve this issue before she returned home? But for the sake of her daughter, she was going to continue applying pressure on him to leave until he understood it.

2 THE PICTURE OF LOVE

Two weeks later

"Here … and take this—you're an unfaithful bastard!" One by one, Clarisse threw out his clothes and belongings into the street as neighbours gathered around to see what was going on. They were all aware of his infidelity, and it did not come as a surprise he was being thrown out of the house. It was her day of reckoning, and she was making it count.

"And don't forget your perfume … I'm sure your mistress enjoyed it!"

One by one, she launched each bottle onto the concrete path—smashing them with the same intent as one would with a Molotov cocktail. She was making a stand, and it was well overdue in the eyes of her family. His possessions were scattered across the street—shirts, pants, underwear and even another woman's bra—it was all there for everyone to see. It resembled a disorganised marketplace with items thrown about and laid derelict on the gravel.

"You should have got rid of that vermin a long time ago!" shouted one of the neighbours.

"You're too good for him, Clarisse," said another woman, pointing at him directly.

There was a sudden round of applause from the crowd of onlookers as he picked up his things and threw them aggressively into his Jeep Renegade car—head down and ashamed by the reaction around him. He was outnumbered and couldn't push anyone around.

In the past, he had relied on his threatening behaviour to silence the people that questioned him. His volatile persona was unpredictable—it meant people turned away from him to avoid confrontation. On this occasion, he was done for, and his powerful broad shoulders, strong chest and six-pack were not going to save him. It was the power of the people: the mob rendered him hapless.

Marlita refused him access to Clarisse at the hospital, and this made him angry. She also asked him to leave home on many occasions, but he had threatened her, preferring to act like a bully instead. However, Clarisse was having none of it—it was her family's house, and he was a boarder, which meant she had rights. Her plan was always to throw him out when she returned home—also, to rally the people in the street for support. She made him aware through gossip what her intentions were—everyone was waiting for the event.

They all knew each other in the street, they made it their business to know what was going on with each family. Generations of different family members grew up in the same house and supported one another during tough times. Clarisse's fiancé was an outsider from another town fifty miles away with a reputation for being a lazy larrikin. How someone as beautiful as Clarisse ended up with such a loser baffled everyone. She knew his tendencies to frighten the neighbours and act aggressively towards them. If they united as a group, there would be nothing he could do—outnumbered and unable to put up a fight, he would have no option but to leave.

"And if I ever see you around here again, I will tear you apart—limb from limb!" Marlita said with a clenched fist. She did not mince her words this time.

He drove off tentatively at first, dodging pieces of stone and gravel thrown on the windscreen by children hidden behind the bushes. The onlookers gestured and made faces at him while one man imitated a gorilla. They wanted to make sure he knew he was not welcome anymore, that their cherished Clarisse would find a better person, one that would respect her and care for her.

The incident with the scarlet chair took its toll on Clarisse and the family. For two weeks she remained in hospital under observation, and the doctors could not diagnose her condition. They ran a series of tests to determine if her condition was part of a more sinister mental condition. But none of the results came back with anything and there was no diagnosed condition. The doctors eventually decided it was related to anxiety and frayed nerves caused by her cheating partner that pushed her to the edge.

The good news was she was at home now and fully recovered with the support of her mother and childhood friend Marjorie. She could not recall the incident with the scarlet chair and Marlita was happy to keep it that way. Those memories and flashbacks would only serve to bring her back to an immobilising state of mind.

After the charade with her fiancé, everyone returned to their normal daily activities, and Clarisse joined Marjorie for an iced tea in the alfresco garden. It was a lovely garden that had been cultivated by her mother since she was a child. It had the best jasmine sambac flowers in the local area—their scent was divine. This beautifully refined white flower bestowed a pleasant jasmine fragrance that provided a calm and relaxing environment. Many family members and neighbours used the garden for afternoon tea and as a time of reflection. Some also picked the flowers to provide a natural scent in their homes—but always made sure there were enough flowers to go around. There was always someone having tea on the old wooden garden table; it became a place for congregation and discussion. All types of problems and family feuds were discussed and resolved around the old wooden table.

"Who are you chatting to on your laptop?" Clarisse asked her friend.

Marjorie smiled and looked directly at her. "Oh, it's just a friend from overseas."

"I didn't know you had a friend from overseas … when did that happen? Must have been when I was in the hospital?"

"I just started talking to him a month ago and he seems nice."

"Oh, so it's a he? Where is he from?"

"Australia."

"It's not a dating site, is it? Come on … I won't tell anyone," Clarisse said.

Marjorie was silent and had a deadpan look on her

face. "It's not a dating site, I got his details from a friend who said he was interested in meeting a girl from the Philippines."

"You don't mean your friend Alicia from Manila? I remember she was always talking about foreign men at work." Clarisse took a sip of her tea. "I think she ended up meeting someone from Australia?"

"Yes, Clarisse, it was Alicia, and she did end up meeting someone from Australia. It was last month, in Manila."

"I thought so. See, I have not lost all my memory."

Marjorie was happy to see Clarisse still had a sense of humour. "Yeah, and he's coming back next month to see Alicia again. I think they care for each other."

"Is he serious about her or just after some fun?"

Marjorie gasped and took a deep sigh.

"Alicia is not that type of girl and you should know her better than that!"

"Marjorie, you know what foreigners are like. You should be more careful with the person you're talking to from Australia."

"I only talk to him about things that I want him to know … nothing more than that. Do you want to see his photo?"

"Yeah, sure. Show me."

She turned her laptop towards Clarisse and clicked on his profile. "So, what do you think?"

"Yeah, he's cute and not that old either. Do you have any more photos?

"Just this one. He sent it today while working on his car."

"Oh, that's nice … the car, I mean."

"Are you being funny, Clarisse?"

"You know me. I am just joking." She took another sip of tea to relieve herself from the stifling heat. "It looks like you got yourself a find, and he is very *guapo*."

"We are just talking." Marjorie was trying to play the whole thing down. "He has a lot of interesting things to say about Australian life."

"Talking is OK, I suppose … it can't hurt if it's long distance." Clarisse glanced at her with a grin. "I mean, he can't just turn up at the front door and give you a hard time."

"Yes, or be demanding and expect things," Marjorie said. "Can I send him your photo? He has a friend that is interested in chatting with someone beautiful like you."

Clarisse jolted and stood upright with her hands on her slender hips. "You want to do what? Send him my photo, just like that?"

There was an excruciating silence as both of them

looked at each other, not knowing what to say next.

"The one in the scarlet chair we took last year during the Day of the Dead—it's a perfect photo of you and you look so sexy."

Clarisse sighed while taking her dark-brown hair and pulling it back into a ponytail—adjusting it until it was dead straight and flawless. It was her way of releasing the tension from her body.

The contours of her dark-brown almond eyes blended into her sculptured face and accentuated her model-like beauty. She inhaled through her nose and out through her mouth ten times, while in deep thought. It was a breathing technique taught to her during her counselling sessions in the hospital to make her feel calm.

Mindfulness, she thought. Mindfulness …

Marjorie waited for her to finish the breathing technique before making any further comments.

"I remember that picture you took last year on the Day of the Dead … have you got it? Can I see it?" Clarisse asked.

Marjorie turned the laptop towards her and said, "This would turn on any guy."

Clarisse pulled the laptop closer to get a better look.

"Hmm, this is not a bad pic at all. I remember it now." She was wearing a short, tight green dress, just above her knees. Legs crossed and her hands together, placed on her thighs—she had a cheeky look that resonated deep into the camera. Her luscious red lips and long fake eyelashes accentuated her gorgeous round face. Her smile told a thousand words and invited you into her beaming presence. Marjorie had been very deliberate in choosing this picture because it was a standout and men would fall all over each other to meet Clarisse.

"So, now that you're finished with your anger … do you want me to send your picture?" Marjorie said.

"I thought I told you I was not interested?"

"He has a single friend, and he keeps asking about meeting a beautiful girl from Manila," Marjorie said.

Clarisse's luscious, full lips broke out in an infectious smile and her face filled with benevolence.

"So, you told them I was beautiful?" Clarisse asked curiously.

"Yes—he asked for a copy of your photo."

"Really! What did you say?"

"I said I would ask you."

Clarisse had gone from exalted anger to controlled optimism in just a few minutes. She was never surprised with Marjorie—always trying something different and testing the boundaries.

"How do you connect with your friend online? Is it

through an application you use—Viber, WhatsApp, or some other chat?"

"Don't mention this to anyone, but it's a dating site."

"What? You want to put my picture on a dating site?" Clarisse choked.

"I don't want to put your picture anywhere."

"Oh, I see." Clarisse finally understood there was no malice.

"Do you want to chat with this guy or not?"

"That's a little soon, don't you think?"

"Well, do you want to think about it then?" Marjorie said.

"How do I chat with him just like that? I don't know him—how do I start the conversation with a stranger?" This type of impromptu chat with a foreigner was new to Clarisse. The courting process in her country was long and formal and getting to know someone was a step-by-step approach.

"Chatting may do you some good, Clarisse, after what you have been through. It's online and easy to turn off—particularly if you don't like the conversation," Marjorie said enthusiastically. She did not feel bound by the informal rules embedded in her culture. Always willing to test the boundaries—but knowing when to stop if she had gone too far.

"I guess there is no harm in it," Clarisse said. Her hair was bouncing into her eyes as a slight breeze of warm air sent petals from the jasmine sambac onto the garden bed. "I suppose nobody needs to know except you, Marjorie … how do you set up a profile?"

"We can do it now if you like. It won't take long, and I already have your photo with me."

"You're very quick off the mark … how about I think about it—we can meet this afternoon?"

"I can prepare your profile and then show you what it looks like later on?" Marjorie was insistent.

Clarisse took another sip of her tea and paused for a while. "Let's wait until this afternoon," she said, still reluctant.

"OK then—it's a plan." Marjorie picked up her laptop and stood up from the garden chair. "Well, I will meet you in a couple of hours then."

"Yeah, sure. I will see you then."

Throughout the afternoon, Clarisse thought about building her profile for the dating site and including photos to raise her appeal. The images looked irresistible and provided snapshots of how beautiful she was—a slender body and a curvature that women would pay lots of money to replicate. Clarisse was so pretty that men could not stop gaping at her. Instead, she ended up with a lousy character who thought he could play around to suit himself without consequences.

Clarisse had become desensitised to the attention of other men. She was not the type that revelled in the attention or counted how many men had shown interest in her. She was not interested in boosting her ego. The issue for Marjorie was how to filter the number of approaches by men seeking a conversation with Clarisse on the dating site.

Although reluctant initially, Clarisse became more accepting of the concept of talking to a man from another country—although she did not like dating sites and Marjorie had to find another way. It offered her the safety of distance and the ability to 'turn off the tap' if that was how she felt. No dates, personal visits, phone calls or commitments to uphold—and it suited her perfectly for now. She was finished with relationships and the infidelity that tagged them. This offered her a way of having conversations with a man without all the responsibilities that went with it.

They met in the garden again, and Marjorie came up with an alternative to the dating site.

"Why don't we create a Skype profile so you can chat and see each other without going through a dating site?"

"You mean like the Skype we use at work to speak to

our office overseas?" Clarisse asked.

"Yes, the same, and that way it's personal—you only contact one another when you want. No public profiles or random messages from people trying to contact you on a dating site."

"I can live with that, Marjorie, because I am in control … and it's not a dating site."

She assisted Clarisse in setting up a private Skype account with words to describe her personality, likes, dislikes—without overdoing it too much. Clarisse demanded a real representation and not a blown-out depiction of someone she wasn't.

"I'm not out to impress anyone—I am who I am, and they need to see me as a normal girl," Clarisse said.

Marjorie agreed to keep the profile as close to her original self as possible. Without her knowledge, Marjorie placed a filter on her profile as to who could contact her. It would be to the advantage of her Australian chat mate.

She was concerned for Clarisse and what she had been through with her fiancé. Setting her up to chat with a man from overseas was part of her strategy. Clarisse needed to move on and forget her past with her tormentor. A long-distance conversation would be harmless—becoming friends with someone from a faraway place may be the distraction she needed.

Marjorie completed the profile, and everything was ready to go. Clarisse tested her login details and cross-checked her credentials to make sure Marjorie wasn't too creative with the content. Marjorie made sure her long-distance friend had the Skype address they needed to send an invitation to Clarisse. Now it was a waiting game—waiting for the invitation to connect. Marjorie informed her to check her email inbox every morning and afternoon to respond to the request when it arrived.

The person that Marjorie introduced to her was called 'Harry'. He was an engineer from Melbourne and worked for the same communication company since he graduated from university. He was about five years older than Clarisse and looked after his fitness and diet. This provided him with youthful looks and the characteristics of someone younger than his age. Like Clarisse, he had also been unlucky in love, and his marriage did not work out. Not because of anything that he had done—it was beyond his control.

Harry had an interest in the history and colonisation of South-East Asia—and read lots of books on the topic. He understood the background of the century's conquest of the Philippines by the Spanish conquistadores. He read about life in Manila—referred to by locals as the 'City of Affection'. He learned how the country became a devoted Catholic one during the years of Spanish influence. He remembered reading a commentary from a historian on the subject: "The Americans gave them the English language, but the Spanish gave them God."

They were profound words that made lots of sense to him at the time.

If anything, Harry would be curious to learn from Clarisse about their culture. He was open-minded when it came to experiencing other cultures. Being a calm person that enjoyed routine, he didn't like taking risks either at work or in his private life. His marriage breakdown made him unsettled and withdrawn from life. The old swagger he used to have was a distant memory and he mainly kept to himself—except for his long-time friend Matt, who was always there to support him.

Marjorie went to get another pot of tea—the dating site was opened and logged into her profile. Clarisse moved the laptop towards her and made a bold move. She decided to access the dating site by pretending to be Marjorie and go for a test run without her knowledge. As she became more acquainted with the navigation links, she searched the profile of her ex-fiancé. Knowing that he would have operated under an alias and probably lied about his age and relationship status, she tried different search criteria that closely linked with his profile. After performing up to ten different searches, she nailed it. There he was—all muscles and wearing no shirt. He posed by flexing his muscles to accentuate the build of his body and six-pack. He had been on this dating site while they were together, she could tell by the month and year that he first set up his profile.

Clarisse was not upset and found it amusing that he would go to such lengths to attract a girl. It also vindicated her feelings that he was no good. For now, she had found undeniable evidence of his infidelity.

She was still feeling apprehensive about chatting with a foreigner on Skype. It was not something she would ever have considered doing in the past—but her life had changed with recent events. She had a different outlook on life. The thought of talking to someone from another country sounded intriguing, but it also made her apprehensive.

3 LONG-DISTANCE RELATIONSHIP

Harry received a knock on the door. It was a courier with a sealed envelope with an official stamp that read 'Harrington's Divorce Lawyers', and he had been expecting it.

I know what this is, he thought.

His relationship had broken down after two years of marriage. It was fine until he got married, purchased a home and they had moved in together permanently. Before they made their commitment to tie the knot it was fun—they lived in separate apartments and maintained flexible work commitments. It did not matter if either of them was away for a couple of days on a business trip. That all changed when they got married and moved in together—as they struggled to keep the same lifestyle and working arrangements they had before.

Perhaps they were both naïve, unrealistic and selfish and never realised it. Harry's wife ramped up her career with a management promotion that required working extra hours and extended travel commitments. She was always in a different city, living out of a suitcase. She was a corporate lawyer attending to quite sophisticated legal matters that required her full dedication and she made them a priority. They had no life outside work and maintaining a relationship via Facetime had a limited lifespan.

It only required one moment of infidelity, vulnerability or drunkenness for their relationship to go sour. His wife woke up one morning in a hotel room next to her boss. It was the result of a drunken escapade after a dinner with clients. She enjoyed his charisma while they regularly travelled together. They spent more time with each other on the road than she did with Harry.

Was it a one-night stand or something else in the making? Harry found out when she came home and told him everything due to the immense feelings of guilt she had developed. She had just cheated on her husband. It was irreconcilable, and it broke his heart. Harry could not get himself to trust her anymore and didn't want to live life thinking about it all the time—they separated and called it quits.

As for the envelope, it was a legal summons to appear in court to settle property and assets. It got ugly—there was no financial settlement in sight. From hope to carnage and love to bitterness—his marriage had become a pariah and a source of deep frustration.

His ex-wife believed he would forgive her transgression and infidelity and they would make a new start together. But she did not want to change anything, preferring to keep her career and lifestyle. Harry wanted nothing to do with it and packed his bags—the relationship was doomed.

His divorce had been a life-changing moment for him; he now held different views about women and relationships. He was not in the same singles market as before—the type of women showing interest in him had a different profile. They were older, stubborn and with high expectations he found difficult to accommodate. They carried terrible habits and baggage from their previous relationships that served as a constant warning. He was not craving love and affection. He wanted to keep to himself.

Harry had arranged to catch up with his best friend Matt at the local café. Matt had returned from Manila two days ago and had lots of stories about his escapades.

The most exciting story was his meeting with Alicia—his chat mate on Skype of almost six months. They caught up in Manila on many occasions, and Matt was excited about her.

The Riverside Café was a popular spot for people living in the local area. It served walkers, runners, bikers and exercise fanatics of all persuasions as an after-exercise retreat. Harry chained his cross-country bike next to the same tree as he had done many times before. He was the type of person that revelled in constant familiarisation with his environment. He would go to the same hotel and beach resort every year and sit on the same spot at the beach. Oh yes, it was his spot, and beware anyone wanting to take it from him!

He noticed Matt sitting at their usual table away from the main bar and facing a large window with a view of the river. He liked this location because it was tucked away and not as noisy.

"Hi, Matt! And? How was Manila? Did it meet your expectations?" They shook hands and took their seats.

"Mate, it was great—I have so much to tell you … so where do I start?"

"You look very refreshed and relaxed. It looks like this holiday did you some good." Harry grabbed the menu and pointed to the list of beers. "Would you like a beer to start with?"

"Yes, that would be great. Are you paying the first round?"

"I will take care of it—but you can pay for the next one." Harry went to the bar to fetch the beer and returned to the table. "So, tell me about the girl … what's her name?

"It's Alicia …"

"Oh yes, Alicia—how did it go with her?"

"She was great. We caught up on three occasions." He took a sip of his beer and wiped his mouth. "She has a wonderful personality and is very pretty."

"I want to know more …" Harry was curious.

"I have a photo of her on my phone. Look—that was taken outside my hotel."

"Well, haven't you done all right for yourself," Harry said. "She has a great smile and looks happy next to you."

"Yes, I must admit when I first saw her, she was stunning. The ash-blonde hair is not her natural colour, but it seems to be very popular. She is always dressed to perfection and presented immaculately."

"What about her personality?"

"Oh, she is so bubbly … likes to joke around and loves to sing karaoke." Matt took a sip of his beer and looked at Harry with sparkling eyes. "Not a bad voice either … she tried to get me to sing—but that wasn't a good move."

"I know you can't sing, Matt."

"It was because I had a few beers that she managed to get me on the microphone!"

"Did you do much else in Manila?"

"Alicia took a day off work and showed me around the tourist sites—it's a big city."

"Are you going to see her again?"

"Yes, I would like to return in the next three months. I will take another week off work and head off to Manila again."

"That sounds promising. I'm happy for you."

"I met her friend Marjorie, and she joined us for dinner one night. They work together in the same company. They both have similar personalities. When they are together, they are very entertaining—one joke after another."

Matt paused for a moment and looked at Harry with a smile. "But that's enough about me, how are you going?'

"Oh, you know, same old shit. Lawyers, court hearings … just one thing after another. I know she is trying to torment me."

"I always find it interesting whether we would marry the same person again if we knew everything about them in advance."

"Like a marriage-warning indicator that can assess future relationships?" Harry said.

"The first person to invent a marriage-warning indicator that works will become a rich person!" Matt said with a cheeky laugh. "Marjorie showed me a photo of her family friend Clarisse, and she is beautiful."

Harry looked at him with a confused expression. "Who is Clarisse again?"

"She is the beautiful woman in the photo I sent to your phone from Manila. You didn't get it?"

"I haven't checked. I'm sure you sent it—I didn't pay too much attention to all your messages because of the problems I have been having with the lawyers. But you never actually met Clarisse?"

"No, just the photo—also what Marjorie explained to me. Maybe you should check the photo because she is stunning—hopefully you haven't deleted it?" Matt sipped on his beer and took a deep breath. "They are not like the girls here."

"What do you mean?"

"They are simple and not pretentious. Always smiling, and in moments of adversity they have their faith and believe everything will turn out fine."

"That sounds refreshing." Harry was becoming interested. "Tell me more?"

"They are close to their families and celebrate special events together. Happy with what they have—don't overspend on things."

"Bargain hunters?"

"Something like that—they are frugal and like to save … although it can be hard making a living on their wage. They don't get paid like you and me."

"I heard they like foreigners because they want our money," Harry said.

"Like any country, you have your gold diggers that can't be trusted—this is where you need to take some precautions and do your due diligence."

"Did you check Alicia before you travelled to Manila?"

"I guess I did ask the right questions while we were chatting and I'm sure she was aware of it." Matt sculled the rest of his beer and took a deep breath. "I suppose I had nothing to lose because I like visiting other countries—at worst she would have been my tour guide and nothing else."

"I see your point … I will check Clarisse's photo when I get back tonight."

"Oh, and don't take too long. The girl is hot property and men are lining up for her."

"She is that pretty?"

"Absolutely, and she has recently set up a profile on

Skype—that might be a good way to start a conversation; it will be low-key." Matt paused and leaned over to him with a fatherly expression. "I understand what you have been through with your marriage breakdown, and your point of view about women at the moment. But chatting is harmless as long as you don't promise anything and keep your money in your wallet."

"What do you mean, Matt?"

"A genuine woman from Manila will not ask you for anything even if they need it—they have pride. Alicia never asked me for anything when I was with her—she even paid her own meal many times."

"Well … that's a good way of finding out their true intent—I will keep that in mind."

As was their custom every time they got together, the steak sandwich was their choice of food accompanied by more beer.

After his meal with Matt, Harry returned home and dashed towards his laptop.

Need to find this photo Matt sent me, he thought.

He opened Matt's messages and searched for the photo. And there she was—the beautiful Clarisse, sitting on an antique scarlet chesterfield chair. He blinked his eyes several times and looked again.

Thank God I did not delete it, he thought.

Her long brown hair, almond eyes and perfectly rounded face supplemented her charismatic smile. She was a beacon for the soul and her looks were mesmerising. The photo was an invitation—a calling card to get to know her intimately. Harry was captivated, and each time he looked at her photo, he would look at it longer and longer. He succumbed and saved her picture as a screensaver before resting his laptop on his bedside table.

Can you fall in love with a picture? he thought.

Harry set up his profile on Skype and searched for Clarisse's details as instructed by Matt. The next step was to send the invitation and wait for the response. According to Matt, she was waiting to be invited to connect and start the conversation. All he had to do was be ready for the reply.

The next morning Clarisse responded with a warm greeting and more photos of herself. He opened the message—it contained a request to chat in one hour.

Should I accept or not? he thought. I'm not ready or presentable.

The clock was ticking, and time was running out—he needed to decide soon.

He went to the bathroom to wash up and looked straight into the mirror. He hadn't shaved for three days and looked scruffy. His hair was messy, it was too long and untidy. He had let himself go because his appearance meant nothing anymore. Harry had given up on women—and the man who once prided himself on his meticulous appearance was a shadow of his former self.

So, what do I do now—look at me, who would find me attractive? he thought.

He turned his face away from the mirror in disgust and then glanced over again at his image. Lowering his head slightly, he clasped his forehead with his left hand while he leaned on the sink. A teardrop of discontent balanced on his right eyelid, and then went rushing down onto the basin below. He was remorseful for what he had become—a desensitised, straightforward sort of guy only interested in his everyday struggles with life.

In a spur of anger, he picked up the first object in front of him, a bottle of Versace Blue Jeans perfume, and threw it against the wall with the force of a wrecking ball—sending pieces of glass smashing in all directions, including the mirror. He placed both hands on his forehead and stood motionless for a while, contemplating what he had just done.

Precisely what she wanted me to become—an out-of-control man that has given up on life, he thought.

His ex-wife was a constant torment to him—she made sure of it. Legal threats, no cooperation and a deep-seated agenda to back him into a corner. She wanted him to bite back like a vicious viper—it gave her absolute satisfaction. Harry was going to have none of it, and from this point on would take back control of his life. He wanted to be the man he once was—the considerate person who believed a problem represented nothing more than a journey to an eventful solution. The positive guy that made others feel happy through his joyfulness, encouragement, and thought-provoking and uncanny expressions.

For the next hour, he cleaned himself up to look respectable again. If he was going to have a live chat with Clarisse on webcam, his appearance had to improve. He was punching above his weight with her beauty. He needed to work on his looks to give himself a chance. Matt had not provided Clarisse with any photos of him, he'd just given her a detailed description of his likes and dislikes. He would need to live up to the well-intended, but exaggerated commentary that Matt had provided to Marjorie.

Harry was logged into Skype waiting for the call from Clarisse. He waited patiently—five, ten, then fifteen minutes and still nothing. He checked the international time zone to make sure it was the right time. Manila was three hours behind during the summer daylight savings time—he was not sure if Clarisse would have allowed for the extra hour.

I think I will make myself a coffee and come back, he thought.

Thirty minutes had passed and still no call. Harry lay back on the chair, scratched his head and sighed. Maybe the information was wrong and the confusion with the time zones added to the complexity. He was not one to blame others—that was not his nature, he always felt there was an explanation for everything. He decided to wait a little longer before calling it quits. Another thirty minutes had passed and still no call. Harry stood up from the chair and put his hands on his side, stretching both sides of his back to remove the stiffness resulting from his seated posture.

Precisely on the hour, he received a message with instructions to click the answer button. Next to the link was a profile photo of Clarisse. He was so captivated by her beauty that he nearly fell under a spell and off his seat—almost forgetting to answer the call.

"Hello, this is Clarisse. Can you see me on your screen?" It was a sweet voice with an American accent.

"Yeah, hi, Clarisse. It's me, Harry. I can see you well. Can you see me?"

"I can hear you, but I can't see you. Do you want to

try clicking on the icon with the webcam?" While he was staring at her video stream, he had forgotten to activate his webcam.

"Oh yeah … I got it. Is that better?" Harry said.

Clarisse smiled as her attractive face appeared in front of his eyes. The image consumed him—he struggled for words. "Harry, I can see you now. It looks like we have made a connection."

"It looks like you're talking to me from the room next door. Isn't that amazing?"

"Same here at my end. You are so clear I can almost touch you." Clarisse smiled, placing her finger on the webcam to simulate the effect.

"I felt that touch." Harry liked her sense of humour.

"I realised when I was calling you that our international clock was wrong and forgot to take into account the extra hour for daylight savings."

"You know about daylight savings?" Harry asked.

"Yes, I work in a call centre—I need to be aware of it for our US callers … they set the clock forward one hour during their summer." She looked directly at the webcam, her piercing almond eyes and long eyelashes emphasised on the screen.

"It's OK, Clarisse, and no bother. Now that we have this down pat it won't be a problem for next time."

"So, Harry … what do you know about me besides the picture you have?"

"Not a lot, other than what my friend who travelled to Manila to meet up with Alicia has told me. He also spoke about Marjorie—how are you and Marjorie related?"

"Marjorie and I are childhood friends—we grew up in the same street. She got me the job in the company some years ago, and we live close to each other here in Manila."

"Well, that explains it …" Harry said.

"What about you and your friend … I have forgotten his name?" Clarisse asked.

"The person who is speaking with Alicia?"

"Yes."

"Oh … that's my best friend Matt and he's the one that gave me your photo." Harry shifted in his chair to make himself comfortable.

"I think they caught up a couple of times while I was in my hometown. But Marjorie told me about him." Clarisse adjusted her wavy hair in front of the webcam and held it back with a band. "It's amazing that I am talking to you—thousands of miles away and connected through a circle of friends."

"The world is becoming smaller all the time—now you can meet people from other parts of the world and not just in your backyard." Harry could see in the webcam video that he was starting to slump over. He adjusted his pose so that he could appear attentive.

"I want to know more about you, Harry. Marjorie did not give me too much information about you."

"Sure, I think I can give you a snapshot of me." He shifted in his chair and leaned forward so that Clarisse could get a better view of him. "My marriage did not work out after two years—I have recently divorced, and I'm single again. I live on my own in an apartment and I work as a consultant for an information technology company."

"Marjorie told me you also like fixing cars?"

"Yes. I bring old cars back to life that are considered collectables. It's more a hobby than anything else."

"Must take a while to bring them back to their original condition?" Clarisse asked.

"Oh yeah—the biggest problem is the lack of spare parts. Once it took me three months to find a small part."

"What happens if you can't find a part?" Clarisse was inquisitive.

"That's when it gets hard and I need to find a way to make it from scratch."

"Wow, I like your hobby, and the car I saw in the picture looks special—a blast from the past."

"I have been asked to use it for weddings—a movie

producer wanted to hire it for a scene in his film."

"You're kidding me?"

"I could make money from it by renting it for special events, but I have never been comfortable with it. I have always wanted to preserve it—keep it pristine."

"I can understand, Harry. You have put a lot of your pride in that car."

"I don't know too much about you, Clarisse—tell me about yourself. My best friend Matt is not always good with the detail."

Their conversation lasted for hours, and they talked about many things—their likes, dislikes, music, sport and their way of life. They tried to stay clear of discussing their past relationships as it always muddied the water. They shared many similarities and points of view that pushed along the discussion. Rarely did they have to stop and think about what to ask each other. The questions flowed effortlessly, one after the other, and sometimes they had to cut each other off to get their say.

Clarisse asked him to connect again the next day on Skype—Harry agreed enthusiastically.

As for Harry, he was over the moon and could not stop thinking about Clarisse after the call. He placed his laptop on his bedside table with Clarisse's Skype profile picture in view. It made him feel comfortable viewing her image while lying down on his bed.

Harry was due to meet Matt the next morning as scheduled—every Saturday at 10 a.m. It was the only time they had to catch up due to their busy lifestyles. Harry, being a man of routine, always chose the same venue and ordered his usual poached eggs on toast. They also sat at the same table facing the window with the river walk view. Matt had given up trying to get him to change cafes because Harry was into this routine.

Upon arrival at the café, they took their usual seats. Matt made a bet with himself that Harry would sit in precisely the same chair facing the window as before.

"So, Harry, did you chat with Clarisse?"

"Yeah … it went perfectly. We spoke for hours and I reckon I could have gone easily for another hour."

"That's promising. Well, she is beautiful, and you're a lucky man."

"Do you mean I could not get anyone like her here?" Harry took offence to his comment.

"That's not what I mean. But it's highly unlikely we could find someone like Clarisse locally. Are you about six years older than her?"

"Yeah, something like that—but I don't focus on it too much because I look after myself. I don't look my age."

"Yes, all that exercising you do does pay dividends when it comes to the opposite sex. But what about her personality?"

"She has an amazing temperament. She smiles a lot, which is also very pleasant—makes me feel like being around her."

"Come to think about it, Harry—your ex-wife never smiled and was very serious," Matt said.

"You noticed that?"

"Yeah, I think we all did. Now that you're divorced—I don't think you will mind me saying she wasn't pleasant to be around."

Harry took a sip of coffee and glanced at the menu. "Yes, mate, it was always about her career, travel and money. Always comparing herself to other people."

"Well, it was meant to be. Let's leave those old memories behind. So, tell me more about Clarisse?"

"Sure, I can talk all day about her."

"By the way, Harry—why are you looking at the menu? You always order the same—poached eggs on toast. If I'm not mistaken, they are on their way right now."

Matt had pre-ordered Harry's breakfast without his knowledge. The rest of the morning was spent talking about Clarisse and how happy he was to have made her acquaintance. He also thanked Matt for being determined as usual to introduce Clarisse to him. Although the photo of Clarisse sitting on the scarlet chair was convincing enough.

While driving home after breakfast, Harry reflected on his friendship with Matt. He had known him since grade school, and they went to the same secondary college and university together. Of all the friendships Harry built throughout his life, Matt was the only mainstay and trusted confidant.

Harry often thought about the saying 'opposites attract': they were uniquely different in many ways. Matt was a sharp-eyed, good-looking lad with heaps of personality. Tall, handsome and a gym junkie with broad shoulders and a six-pack to boot. Never married or tied down to anyone—he carried a free spirit. He was always travelling to exotic locations no one had heard of, and his stories were amazing.

Harry trusted Matt and his views on girls—if the recommendation was positive, then rest assured, Matt had done his homework.

4 THE CITY OF AFFECTION

Three months later

Harry had a pleasant flight from Melbourne to Manila, arriving in the afternoon and during the warmest part of the day. He left his hometown in the middle of spring to a sharp change in temperature awaiting him outside the airconditioned airport. It had been raining before his arrival—it was hot and humid. Just standing around without any exertion made you swelter and sweat profusely—a stickiness that made your clothes cling to your skin like plastic wrap.

Clarisse was waiting at the arrivals area of the international airport with Marjorie—she had accompanied her to help find Harry and welcome him. She had never travelled outside the country before and having Marjorie's support helped her confidence. She was conscious of meeting a foreign guy for the first time after chatting with him for the past three months on Skype. It was a long-distance relationship—an 'LDR' as Marjorie would put it. It dawned on her this was the real McCoy—the genuine thing, face to face. It was nerve-racking just thinking about it—her stomach churned at the sight of every foreign-looking man walking through the arrival's door. One by one, the passengers passed by with their luggage trolley stacked full. She stood on her toes like a glancing ballerina—looking between the shoulders of others to get a glimpse of Harry.

Finally, she recognised him in the distance. Harry was all smiles but bewildered as he looked around, searching for Clarisse. They had agreed he would wear a blue Adidas hoodie and denim straight-leg pants so that she could recognise him. Clarisse waved frantically and bounced up and down, creating an exercise of movement so he could identify her.

"Over here, Harry … I'm over here," she said. Clarisse was so loud that everyone turned around and glanced at her.

Harry spotted her and his face lit up, smiling enthusiastically but also relieved that he had made it. He pointed to Clarisse and mimed to her like a pantomime.

He was on his way towards her as he juggled suitcases, other passengers doing the same thing. As he reached the gate leading to the visitors' area, Clarisse dashed towards him and gave him a big hug, causing the luggage to fall off the trolley in front of prying eyes.

"Finally, I have made it," Harry said.

"I can't believe you're here."

"Now, isn't this better than Skype?" Harry smirked.

"So, you're wearing the blue hoodie I asked you to wear."

"Three other guys were wearing similar blue hoodies— I thought you might run towards the wrong person?"

Clarisse was accustomed to his dry sense of humour and smiled. She used to get it all the time during their Skype conversations—it always made her feel cheerful.

"You're taller than you appear on webcam," she said.

"Webcams can be deceiving, but not in your case— you look terrific as always, Clarisse, if not better."

She blushed and nodded her head down like a shy teenager. "Thank you so much for your compliment."

"So, where do we go from here?" Harry said.

"Marjorie is over there … see her waving?" Clarisse pointed towards the taxi rank. "She has a private cab that will take you to your hotel."

"Oh, that's great … I had a bumpy flight, and I feel

lightheaded from the jet lag."

A security officer tapped Harry on the shoulder and informed him that his luggage had fallen off his trolley—blocking the path. The thrill of meeting Clarisse on top of his tiredness meant he had forgotten entirely about his luggage. He apologised and carefully restacked the suitcases.

Clarisse took the lighter carry-on bag and helped Harry towards the cab. Inside the cab, Clarisse positioned herself in the backseat between Marjorie and Harry with the excuse she could talk to both. They got underway and left the chaos of the airport through the congested Manila streets. He was awestruck by the number of people covering the roads and pathways—it was a constant procession of folk going about their business. And forget about the cars driving in an orderly fashion in a straight line as they did back home—he was in a zig-zag world. Every inch of space counted if you wanted to get home in a reasonable time.

As the cab pushed its way through the dense traffic and manoeuvred side to side, Harry could feel the warmth of Clarisse's body at every turn. Her Versace Crystal Noir perfume filled the cab with a sexy fragrance designed to arouse men uncontrollably. And although he was tired from the flight, he didn't mind at all—it was a side effect of the traffic congestion that brought them together at each turn.

Clarisse apologised for the time it was taking to get to the hotel, but he shrugged it off and smiled. Harry was happy to spend extra time with Clarisse and talk about the last three months. There was so much to discuss that they took turns recounting their previous conversations—most of it was small talk and clarifying unfinished dialogue.

"Well, there you are Harry, the Novotel Hotel," Clarisse said.

"Finally here, I can't wait to get some rest."

"So, we will see you tomorrow after work. How does 8 p.m. suit you?"

"Oh, that's fine. I will get to sleep in, go to the hotel gym and then get ready to see you," Harry said.

"I will message you the details of where to meet me. It's not far from here."

"Sure. And thanks for picking me up, I appreciate it."

"Have a good night, Harry." Clarisse kissed him on the cheek and waited while the driver unloaded his bags and handed them to the porter.

Harry checked into the hotel and dropped off his backpack to his room. He decided to have a light beer in the lobby bar to calm down before heading off for bed.

The lobby bar was vibrant with lots of foreigners having drinks with their spouses. Across the table, directly in front of him, was a man in his late fifties, on his own and enjoying a light ale.

"Your girlfriend is stunning, mate," he said, looking directly at Harry.

"You mean *my* girlfriend?" Harry wasn't sure if the comment was directed towards him or another person.

"Yes, the girl in the green floral dress. You were in a cab with her."

"Oh yes, I met her today for the first time—but we have been chatting for months." He took a sip of his beer and then sighed.

"Long-distance relationship, hey? We all start like that, you know." He smiled at Harry and then walked over to his table. "Nice to meet another Aussie in the City of Affection."

"Likewise. Why don't you take a seat? By the way, why do you call it the City of Affection? I have heard that a few times already."

"Most of the men come here looking for love. You know, failed relationships back home and seeking someone special."

"Yes, that's me in a nutshell." Harry had a smirk on his face.

"They call it the City of Affection because it's a mysterious place—there are lots of superstitions amongst the beautiful women. Your partner will drive you nuts over it … just some friendly advice for you from an old man."

"Thanks, I appreciate your advice—my girlfriend has a superstition about a red chair, and I don't understand it. She doesn't want to talk about it," Harry said.

"I would leave it alone if I was you. If you start to dabble in it too much, it will absorb you—don't go there and stay clear of the superstition."

"Yeah … I guess you're right."

"Their culture is very superstitious, and they even have a word for it. Your partner will tell you what you must do to avoid bad luck. You will get fed up with it—there is nothing you can do. Goes with the territory."

"That's good to know because I'm spending the next five days in Manila and I may be visiting her family."

"Well if it makes you feel any better, I went through all of that ten years ago—I'm still married. I was divorced before and am happily married now." He stood up and waved across the room to his wife. "Better go, she has returned from shopping and looks tired."

"OK, mate, I will see you around."

"Sure. Oh, and one word of advice … treat her like

royalty if you want to win her heart."

"Thanks for the tip-off, mate. Have a good night. Might see you around the hotel some time?"

"Sure thing."

Harry called it a night and went to his room to rest up.

Clarisse agreed to meet Harry on her own at a shopping precinct near her work. She was finishing her shift around 8 p.m.; it was vibrant in central Manila as the locals headed off for dinner around this time. And why wouldn't you? It was always a warm, pleasant evening with lots of people walking about—spending time together in the restaurants that walled the Greenbelt shopping complex from one side to the other. The atmosphere at the complex—an open mall with an outdoor church located in the heart of the precinct—was lively at this time of the evening.

Getting to the mall from his hotel was easy as he navigated through the central business district to get to his location. It took Harry about ten minutes to arrive on foot—he didn't mind dodging people on the overflowing footpaths. The charm of the city absorbed him along the way as he took in all the sights and sounds.

Even though he enjoyed the company of her friend Marjorie at the airport yesterday, he was looking forward to meeting the beautiful Clarisse on their own. There was only so much you could talk about when your friends were around. The discussion was mainly small talk with a lot of banter. But he liked Clarisse's nature and attitude towards life. If she had problems, you would not know it. Even in times of adversity, she would rise above the shadows to put on a cheerful face. She was a pillar of happiness—she was vibrant, funny and always wore an infectious smile that lit up her face. How could you not embrace her charismatic charm? Harry wanted to be around her all the time and not let her go for an instant.

He waited at a crowded bench just across from the meeting place where Clarisse had given him directions to in a poorly worded text message.

I hope I got this right? he thought.

He looked around for Clarisse, trying not to make it too visible. He was a good-looking guy with a trimmed beard, a Christian Ronaldo haircut and a sculptured face—he may have been a darling catch for the lovely ladies walking past. They took turns looking at him, and some smiled as they casually passed him—deliberately slowing down at first to get a glimpse.

Somewhere in the crowd of people filling the area, he managed to catch a glimpse of Clarisse from a distance, wearing a tangerine dress with motifs of tropical flowers above her knees. He waved and smiled enthusiastically, looking directly at her—but she did not see him at first. He tried again by raising his tall posture to gain an advantage as she was drawing nearer. He could not help notice her slender and perfectly shaped body and skinny legs. She looked terrific, and he was excited to see her again. Like most of the girls in Manila, Clarisse dressed impeccably and always presented herself with expertly applied makeup to accentuate her looks.

Clarisse finally acknowledged him with a brilliant smile and a ferocious wave as she tiptoed, swerving amongst the endless stream of people walking past her to get his attention. She did not yell out his name this time like she did at the airport and was more contained. Eyes fixed and without losing sight of him, she made her way nearer until they were close enough to acknowledge each other.

"Hi, Clarisse, I nearly lost you in that crowd." He wasn't sure whether to shake her hand or leave the formalities out of it. "Does it always get this busy on a Monday night?"

She wiped away any anxiety he had about greeting her by kissing Harry on the cheek.

"Oh, this is normal … wait until Friday night, it's twice as crowded," Clarisse said.

"I'm glad you found me. I was concerned I had the

wrong place and your message …"

"My message was not clear? I realised later that you were not local and that I could have been clearer. I'm sorry … but guess what—you made it!"

Harry was conscious of staring at her and did not want to make it obvious. But he could not help being taken by her presence.

"It's OK, and I had fun getting here … dodging the never-ending rows of people." Harry pointed across the walkway to a bustling café. "Is that the place we should get a table?"

"Yes, I know the food there, and the coffee is great. I'm assuming you like coffee?"

"Oh yeah. The stronger the better for me." There was a table on the perimeter of the café with less noise. Harry briskly made his way towards the table while instinctively clasping Clarisse's hand. It was an impromptu reaction—she didn't mind and went along with it.

"This is a perfect location," Clarisse said. She took a seat and looked at a torn menu that had seen better days.

Before Harry could adjust his seat, a middle-aged woman holding a basketful of coloured roses tapped him on the shoulder. She had been watching him and waiting to pounce.

"Why don't you buy the beautiful girl a flower and

show your true desire for her?" she said.

Harry looked at her with a grin at best, not wanting to be impolite in front of Clarisse. "Oh yes … how much for this red one?"

"Does the price matter, sir? The beautiful girl next to you is priceless, and many men are waiting to be where you are seated right now."

He was gobsmacked. This woman knew her lines and how to make a foreigner look pitiful in the eyes of a beautiful woman. He had to think quick to get the upper hand and redeem himself.

"I know, why don't you choose one, Clarisse?" He paused and waited for a reaction. "Go on … they are all nice roses, I don't know which one to select."

Clarisse had seen this woman up to her old tricks before. Preying on local women dating foreigners and skilfully extracting the sale from embarrassed men like Harry.

"I like the red rose … can I have that one?"

"Yes, of course." Harry pointed to the red flower in the basket. "That one will do," he said to the woman.

Clarisse took the rose and held it up to her nose before laying it in front of her. "Thank you so much—I wasn't expecting a rose today."

"I hope it will remind you of our special occasion."

"What occasion is that?"

"Oh, don't you remember? Today is the same day of the month we chatted on Skype for the first time."

Clarisse was silenced and didn't know what to say. She had completely forgotten. "It's our monthiversary! Thank you so much, Harry, for your thoughts—what a way to celebrate with a beautiful-smelling rose." Clarisse recovered from her lapse of memory.

"This rose will eventually dry out and wither away—but the memories will last an eternity." Harry was not a great poet, but the words came out naturally.

They both remained silent for a minute and enjoyed the moment. Clarisse was superstitious—the flower was more than just a thoughtful gesture. It was meant to be, and the woman who sold them the rose was not a coincidence.

"That chair you're sitting on in the photo, it looks like an antique." Harry looked straight into her almond eyes and didn't blink.

"Oh yes, I remember that photo—that's the first pic I sent you. Of all the photos you have of me, I'm surprised that's the one you remember the most."

"It's not important—it's only a chair."

"No, tell me. What is it about the chair you found curious … or was it the person sitting on it that took your fancy?" Clarisse smiled and then paused. She wanted an answer and was not going to give up easily.

"Well, it's the colour, to be honest—never seen a chair in that colour before."

"You're very attentive for a male." She adjusted her posture and leaned forward. "I don't often get asked that question, but since you asked nicely—it's a variation of scarlet."

"I thought scarlet was an old woman's name?"

"I think you have been watching too many movies, Harry—by the way, it's made of old-fashioned, genuine leather."

"How old is it?"

"It belonged to my great-grandmother, Elena, and it's been in the family ever since—for generations." Her face lit up with a childish smirk as she gazed into the distance.

"It has a special place in your family?" Harry wanted to know more.

"It's an antique chesterfield chair—almost a hundred years old." Clarisse avoided the question entirely.

"How have you managed to keep it in such good condition?" Harry tried to keep the conversation of the chair going.

"We don't use it every day … just on the anniversary of Elena's death—on the Day of the Dead." She turned to him and chose her words carefully. "My great-grandmother passed away in that chair during her sleep at the age of ninety-two."

He could see the emotion in her eyes and was sympathetic. "That's a tragedy … I mean, to pass away in your sleep on your favourite chair."

"That's why we don't sit in the chair,' she laughed. "I don't want to be the next one to go."

"That's what I love about your country … so many traditions. And the Day of the Dead—what day is that?"

"It's the first and second day of November—we also call it *Día de Los Muertos*. It's a big celebration here."

"That's two days away! So what do you do on this day with the chair? Do you sit on it and that's it?" It all sounded very mysterious to Harry.

"According to what my mother taught me, it's the only day we can sit on the chair." She paused for a moment. "Back in my great-grandmother's day, the scarlet leather chair was a difficult piece of furniture to make until she found a craftsman. It was a labour of love, and it became her prized possession. Maybe one day I will tell you more about the chair. If we get the chance, I can show it to you. It means a lot to my family, and like most Filipinos, we're superstitious."

"I understand your point. Where I come from, we

don't have that sort of culture and old chairs are thrown out and recycled at antique shops—if they have any value. So, when can I see the chair? I'm intrigued by your story."

"Not so fast, Harry. One day." She passed the menu to him in an attempt to change the topic.

"My mother doesn't like people outside the family sitting on the chair—so we have to do it when she is not around."

"Really?"

"Yes, she's very superstitious." She passed the menu to him, pointing to the top of the page. "If you can make any sense of this torn menu maybe we can order some food … I'm hungry," Clarisse said.

"There are lots of choices—I would like to try out the local cuisine. Can you pick one and surprise me?"

"I think I can do that. I will order you something with beef, is that OK?"

"Sure."

She took back the menu and said, "It may be quicker if I go and order at the counter." As Clarisse was about to leave Marjorie came jostling by and greeted her fervently.

"Marjorie, what are you doing here?" Clarisse said.

"I was on my way home." She turned and looked at Harry. "Oh, hello, Harry."

"Hi, Marjorie. Nice to meet you again," Harry said.

"Why don't you both get acquainted again while I place our order ... won't be long," Clarisse said.

Marjorie took her seat next to Harry while fiddling with her bag—she did not want to place it on the ground and held on to it. She looked at Harry in a shy way and said, "I don't want to get my new bag dirty ... I only got it yesterday."

"Oh, I see. I thought you were superstitious for a moment." Harry was trying out his dry humour. "So, how long have you known Clarisse?"

"Long time—since I was five years old. Our mothers are best friends, and I got her the job in our company."

"That's a long time. So, you must know a lot about her."

"I'm not going to tell you all her secrets—you will need to work that out for yourself." She paused and turned directly to Harry with her piercing brown eyes. "You know, every man in the office is after her—even the married ones."

"And?" Harry was curious.

"She stays clear of them. Some people think she is a man-hater ... but I think she does not find them interesting. She has been unlucky in love and cautious about any approaches."

"Oh, that's good to know." Harry thought Clarisse

being a man-hater may benefit him in an odd way.

"So, it's your first real time together—what have you been talking about?" Marjorie was forthright and the prying type. It's how she got the information that made her the office gossip.

"We talked about the photo she posted on her Skype profile … the one that caught my eye. When I think about it—it's the main reason I am here. She is beautiful in that photo."

"Was it the photo of her sitting in the scarlet chair?"

"Yes, how did you know?" Harry was beginning to sense that Clarisse had been keeping her updated. "We briefly talked about the chair today—but I don't think it's her favourite topic."

"You're lucky she provided you with that photo because she can only sit in the chair once a year—on the Day of the Dead."

He briefly glanced across the tables in front of him and caught a view of Clarisse placing the order from the café window. He said, "That doesn't make sense … sitting in a chair once a year?"

"It's only superstition—every family has their strange beliefs, and some take it more seriously than others," Marjorie said with a grin.

Harry sat back in the chair and kicked out his feet.

Although he was not the superstitious type, the talk about the red chair had piqued his interest. He did not want to be probing—but he wanted to know more.

"Yes, Clarisse mentioned the first of November—I will be in Manila. I'm leaving the day after, in the evening."

"Hopefully she will invite you to her family celebration of the dead? The cemetery is two hours' drive from here."

Harry looked at Marjorie and was silent, not knowing what to say next. "I would love to be with Clarisse on her family day and share the experience."

"Oh, I made that sound so dreary—in our custom, only people that are close to the family are invited to the celebration of the dead."

"It will be my privilege to attend," he said hopefully.

As Clarisse made her way back to the table, he was conscious of his appearance, instinctively combing his fingers through his hair while straightening his collar.

Marjorie leaned closer to him, cupped her hand in front of her mouth and whispered, "Be careful of her mother—she does not have a good track record with the men Clarisse has brought home in the past." Marjorie turned sideways to avoid Clarisse's glare. "And you being a foreigner isn't going to help either."

He did not know how to take the advice from

Marjorie. Was she trying to warn him and scare him away? If so, why? By the time he could evaluate her comments further, Clarisse was at the table.

"I got our order ... and yes, I got you something too, Marjorie," she said.

The evening was full of laughter and banter. Clarisse had a wicked sense of humour—Harry found her exciting to be around. The more he got to know her, the greater his admiration. Many times, he pinched himself, thinking it was a dream.

Marjorie stayed for a little longer but had to leave to get up early the next morning. Harry could see from the corner of his eye that she signalled to Clarisse with an OK gesture. He presumed it was about himself but did not want to assume anything.

Harry gently kissed Clarisse on the cheek and said goodbye. She invited him to the Day of the Dead celebration with her family. He was excited and apprehensive at the same time—and not sure what to expect. Clarisse did not discuss the chair again and he did not raise the topic either. He sensed it was a touchy subject, and anyway, he would see the scarlet chair at her family celebration tomorrow.

On his way back to the hotel room, he could hear the congregation singing in the background. An open-air

Catholic church in the heart of a shopping centre was unheard of back home. The priests scheduled mass every hour and would change over to ensure the best experience for worshippers. It was well organised and provided continuity from one service to another. People observed the mass on their way home from work. He stopped temporarily to have a look and noticed it was packed with worshippers, with standing room only. A young girl handed him an envelope to make an offering to the church and moved on to another person. Harry grew up as a Catholic—it was all routine for him.

Harry attended the private Catholic school system until he graduated from university. He continued attending mass regularly until he got married and lost connection with his faith. It's not that he gave up on his faith—having an atheist partner who refused to marry in the church made him lose touch with his upbringing. His ex-wife would criticise him for going to mass. She thought it was a complete waste of time—although she had no issue working until late each night to further her career. Her faith was the church of work and career ambition rolled into one. Harry had told her many times her church was the workplace—that her company constituted her religion. It was just one of the many complex incompatibilities of his marriage that gradually pulled them apart.

Harry stood at the back of the church with a slanted view of the ceremony. He was daydreaming about his childhood when he attended church with his parents. It was a nice feeling and he could remember growing up with lots of hugs and kisses. His dad liked taking them for pizza after mass for a family treat.

What he would do to relive those moments again. It brought back fond memories—making him feel at peace while listening to the church choir.

5 DAY OF THE DEAD

It was the first of November and the Day of the Dead—*Día de Los Muertos*. It was going to be a day of celebration and Clarisse was on her way to pick up Harry from the hotel.

Harry made his way to the hotel foyer and sat on the art-deco sofa waiting for her. Time passed by, and she had not arrived—she was running 45 minutes late, and no Clarisse in sight. He was starting to get fidgety, pacing up and down the foyer before sitting down again. There were no messages on his iPhone—this made him feel highly strung.

"You have been waiting for her a while?" said an elderly woman sitting opposite him.

Harry did know how to respond as was caught off

guard. "Yes, she's nearly one hour late and I'm not sure what to do?"

"This is normal—you don't need to worry."

"Really?"

The older woman provided him with a dose of optimism.

"She is testing you … to see how much you care about her. She will make you wait—deliberately. It might feel odd to foreigners like yourself, but in our country, men expect it."

"So, they just wait?"

"Oh yes. They don't complain either. If you love the girl—then you wait."

"I wasn't aware—I wish I'd known." He felt as though he missed something culturally significant.

"Oh, and one other thing—I hope you didn't ask her to meet you in the foyer in public view?"

"Yes, I did."

The older women leaned closer and gazed at him.

"She is probably feeling uncomfortable meeting you in the foyer of an international hotel. She is concerned about the people around you—what they may say about her. You know—meeting a foreigner in a hotel lobby can be misconstrued as something else. Does that make sense?"

"I think I know what you're trying to say. I should

have asked her to meet across the road in a more discreet location. Maybe a quiet café or something like that."

The older woman smiled and nodded her head.

"Oh, must go now, my driver has arrived—and by the way, she expected you to know this but has forgiven you because you're not a local." She grabbed her designer bag from the sofa and waved goodbye. "It's been a pleasure to meet you, and I hope everything works out. You seem like a nice guy."

He had received a lesson in etiquette and realised relationships were more complex in this country. He understood why Clarisse was running late and blamed himself for not researching the local customs. He sat back on the sofa and took a deep breath and ordered a coffee to pass the time.

Another thirty minutes passed when the concierge approached him.

"Sir, I have a message from a Miss Clarisse … I assume you're Harry?"

"Yes, I am." Harry feared the worse— that he might not get to join Clarisse for the Day of the Dead celebration.

"She asked if you can walk across the road to the Vogue Café and meet her there. I can point you in the right direction if you like?"

Harry felt a sigh of relief and exhaled a deep breath. "Sure, that would be perfect. Thank you."

Harry looked across the road and could see the signage of the Vogue Café. He crossed a busy intersection with no traffic lights—dodging cars from all directions. He had to be quick, or he would be stuck there for a long time.

Finally managed to get across this damn road, he thought.

Directly in front was the Vogue Café—a charming French provincial-style café in the heart of the central shopping complex. As he got closer, Clarisse waved to him from the window with an alluring smile. Each time Harry met with her, the splendour of her looks captivated him even more. He had never felt like this before and was struggling to deal with this new emotion.

Before taking his seat, he greeted Clarisse with a kiss on the cheek.

"Are you going to sit down?" she asked.

"Oh yes. You look great today in that stunning dress. I like the colour of jade and the flowering prints—are they depictions of a local tropical white flower?"

"Thank you so much, Harry, it's *sampaguita,* our national flower—we also call it 'jasmine sambac'."

"I'm sorry about asking you to meet me in the foyer of the hotel … not a good place to meet someone special."

"That's OK; it's more intimate here at the café." She adjusted her chair closer to Harry and smiled. "Did an old lady come and speak to you in the foyer, by any chance?"

"Yes, she did, how did you know?"

"That was my aunty—I sent her there to stop you worrying. She also wanted to see you and kept insisting."

They both looked at each other and laughed. Harry had received a lesson on proper etiquette from her aunty.

"Let's quickly grab something to eat and leave … the bus is leaving in forty-five minutes—it's a two-hour trip to my mother's house."

"Does she know I'm coming with you?"

"She knows of you …" Clarisse paused for a moment. "It won't be a problem. You can meet the rest of my relatives at the same time."

Harry gulped and nearly choked on his glass of water because of meeting all her family. It was going to be an exciting day—he decided to go with the flow. He was sure Clarisse had everything in hand, and it would be an eventful day.

They finished breakfast and dashed to the bus terminal about 500 metres away, walking at a steady pace. Clarisse had booked first-class tickets. This service was in high demand—she did not want to lose her seat. When they arrived at the terminal, they barely had time to buy refreshments for the trip before boarding the bus. The two-hour journey was going to be the perfect time to explore a variety of conversational topics—and once they got going, you had no chance of stopping either of them.

"So where exactly is your hometown from here?" Harry said.

"It's south of the city—you won't see too much countryside until we are about one hour's drive from here."

"We have lots of time to talk then."

"And what do you want to talk about first?" Clarisse adjusted her backpack in front of her seat to make room for her slender legs.

Harry could not help noticing her perfectly aligned body and knee-high dress. "We can talk about your family so that I know what to expect when we arrive."

"OK, that's a good idea. Let me give you a brief explanation of who you are likely to meet—there is my mother, Marlita, and she can be testing on men; she will ask you a lot of questions. Then there is my aunty and Uncle Pablo from across the road, and they are a lovely couple. My uncle Pablo is the one that takes us everywhere with his motorbike and sidecar. There is my other aunty whom you have already met at the hotel—she is the outgoing one, always entertaining to have around, the life of any party. You have met Marjorie already so no need to comment about her."

"I'm not sure if I asked you this before—is Marjorie related?"

"Marjorie's mum and dad are my godparents—so in our culture we automatically become related."

"Your mother worries me …"

Clarisse put her hand on Harry's shoulder to comfort him. "Don't worry about my mother … and what is that saying? 'Her bark is worse than her bite'." Clarisse looked at him with a piercing smile.

Harry tilted his head down, trying to imitate a puppy face. It was his dry sense of humour and Clarisse liked it. "I'm sure I can manage your mum somehow …"

"Oh, I forgot to mention. I have three younger cousins—all girls. I think my uncle Pablo gave up trying to have a boy and stopped at three."

"What about your grandparents?"

"They have passed away—we will visit their graves this afternoon as part of the Day of the Dead celebration." Clarisse reached for her bag and pulled out her wallet with an old family picture in black and white. "This was me when I was only five years old with my mother when she was younger."

"I can see where you got your beauty from—your

mother was also a good-looking woman," Harry said.

"Yes, men would do anything to court her in the town—my grandfather had a hard time managing it."

"I can understand why." Harry was trying to pull his seat into an upright position but was struggling to get the release button working.

"You are the only child in your family?"

"Yes, I grew up an only child, but I never felt alone."

She paused for a moment to think about her next words. "My father left us when I was born—I have never met him."

"Oh, that's a sad story," Harry said. He felt he had carelessly brought up a touchy subject and did not want to take it further. He tried to change the subject, but Clarisse stayed with it.

"We can talk about this, Harry; I have had a whole life to adjust to it, so it's OK."

"I appreciate that, but we can talk about something else. So, what else do I need to know about?"

"My younger cousins may rest their forehead on your hand to show respect."

"Something you would do with royalty."

"Maybe in your country but here it is a sign of respect for older people … it means they are asking for your blessing."

"Oh. Well, at least I'll know what it's about," Harry said with a grin.

The conversation continued for well over an hour until Clarisse felt tired and rested her head on his shoulder. Within a couple of minutes, her eyes started to droop and then close completely. Harry turned to have a look—she was well asleep. He had been longing to be close to her and had another hour to enjoy the warmth of her touch. Sitting on a bus next to each other for two hours had brought them closer. And more importantly for Harry, he was starting to have feelings for her.

The bus drove by the crowded cemetery on the way to the bus terminal at a walking pace to avoid the large number of families crossing the road haphazardly. There was a procession of people streaming in from everywhere bearing flowers, religious artefacts and token gifts for relatives that had passed away. The congregation of people was so large that traffic had to be coordinated by the law enforcement officers so the bus could get through.

Around the corner from the cemetery was the entrance of the Catholic church of Saint Ignacio, a historic church influenced by Spanish architecture and built during the period of colonisation. Clarisse explained that church sermons were held every hour to accommodate the stream of people making their way to the cemetery. It was customary to pray for the dead before visiting the cemetery to pay homage. She talked about her mother frequently and how very religious and superstitious she was—growing up with traditional and credulous beliefs as a child.

He asked about the scarlet chair and whether that formed part of the superstition when she was growing up. Clarisse acknowledged the scarlet chair was a problem and it mystified her mother, like an enigma. Harry could sense it was not her preferred conversation topic and decided to leave it for the time being.

The bus arrived at the terminal, and it was only a short five-minute walk to the house she had grown up in. They did not see many foreigners in the town, which meant Harry bore the brunt of the curious stares. Although it was harmless, it made him feel important because nobody bothered paying any attention to him back home. Harry relished it and considered it unusual to be the centre of attraction.

Her mother and relatives greeted them upon arriving at the house; they had been congregating there all morning preparing food and waiting for Clarisse. There were several homes all lined up close together off the main street. They were simple structures built in the traditional stone manner and with tin roofs. No fences separated the homes, and it was unclear where the boundaries were, or perhaps it did not matter as they were all related anyway. Many dogs walked around casually and unimpeded, living off the scraps and generosity of the locals.

Behind one house was a chicken pen with a bounty of eggs collected and left in a basket for the families to take. It was an honour system, and families only took what they needed. In the house further down the stone driveway was a piggery that had an atrocious smell when the wind blew in their direction. Clarisse mentioned the smell got worse during feeding time when the pigs rolled in the mud. Next to Clarisse's home was a small plot of land where they grew all types of vegetables and it was being tended to by older people. The herbs were picked and put into cane baskets. A variety of local vegetables were available for families along this pebbled driveway to choose. Everyone supported each other with whatever produce they had to share.

Harry was unsure whether they knew he was coming—but it did not seem to matter as they took an instant liking to him. The younger children were shy and poked their heads through the door, momentarily trying to catch a glimpse of him.

"I told my mother you like the sampaguita flower and she has them growing in the garden. Want to see them?"

Clarisse said.

"Sure, it would be nice to see them in a real garden."

As they made their way to the back of the house, they heard a rattling on the wooden floor coming from the last room. It sounded like someone was scraping furniture around the house. As they got closer to the backroom with the scarlet chair, the sound resonated again—although this time it was more intense with an eerie feeling. Harry could see the chair was in the middle of the room—it had an unwelcoming presence. The polished scarlet leather had intricate stitching and the chair had ornate, carved wooden legs. There were no windows and barely enough filtered light to fill the room. A dim lamp on a round side table offered some visibility from where they were standing.

Clarisse was holding Harry's arm and tugged on it while escorting him out to the garden.

"Who are all those people in the photo frames on the console table next to the chair?" Harry said.

"Those pictures are family members that have passed away: my grandmother, grandfather, great-grandmother and my two uncles."

"Can I see their pictures?"

"Oh no, we don't need to go in there. The only reason this room is open today is that it's the Day of the Dead—

my mother wants their spirits to be free."

"What about the scarlet chair?"

"That chair was Elena's—we keep it there in memory of her."

"Your great-grandmother?"

Clarisse was clearly feeling uncomfortable and tugged on Harry's arm again. "Yes. Come on, let's go and see the flowers," she said.

As she whisked Harry away from the room, another scraping sound resounded behind them. He did not want to make a fuss even though it raised his suspicion. He continued into the garden to see the range of tropical white lilies.

"See those white flowers growing on a vine ... they are sampaguita and ready to pick. We need about twenty of them to take to the cemetery," Clarisse said. She got the basket and handed it to Harry. "The sampaguita is the traditional white flower with a soft yellow centre."

"They look perfect—your mother has done a great job maintaining them."

"It's a hobby for my mother. She spends a lot of time in the garden manicuring the sampaguita." She grabbed Harry's arm, tugging him gently towards another plant with maturing flowers. "Did you know that the sampaguita flower is a symbol of love and devotion?"

"Oh, so it's a flower you give to someone you care about …" Harry picked the best flower from the vine and smelled its fragrance before handing it to Clarisse. "Here, this flower is for you. I'm so happy to be here on this special day. Thanks for inviting me."

Clarisse squinted her eyes and smiled. "Thank you so much." It seems she was beginning to see the caring side of him.

"It reminds me of a perfume, but it won't come to me," Harry said.

"Did you know that the fragrance of Lady Gaga's perfume 'Fame' was thought to be inspired by sampaguita? Her inspiration came from when she bought one from a street child on the road in Manila."

"I had no idea that is what inspired her. I think that is the perfume I was referring to before, 'Fame'," Harry said.

"We have enough flowers now, so I will tie them and put them in the basket. I need to give some to the family members because they always expect my mother's flowers on the Day of the Dead to take to the cemetery."

As they walked to the front of the house, they passed the room with the scarlet chair again. Harry briefly looked inside but could not see anything unusual. This time he managed to admire the design and craftsmanship of the chair. Back home, it would have been a sought-after antique because of its pristine condition and craftmanship. It was an elegant piece of furniture from a time when character, charm and design were of utmost importance. Chairs like these were designed to last and not be thrown out after five years.

They don't make furniture like that anymore, he thought.

They headed off to church to have their flowers blessed and to pray for the dead. The mass would last around forty-five minutes; he was not sure how to follow the mass rituals. Clarisse assured him not to worry and to sit there patiently, there were no expectations.

After the church ceremony, they took the sampaguita flowers to the cemetery to pay homage to Clarisse's relatives by laying the flowers next to their graves. They were all laid to rest at the same gravesite, occupying tombs next to each other. Generations of the family lined up in a row from the oldest grave to the most recent. The graves were so close together that not an inch of spare ground was left. Some graves had up to five family members in them, to maximise room in a congested cemetery that was overflowing. Harry had to be careful not to step on anyone's grave as they moved around from one headstone to another. Her family's graves went back generations to her great-grandparents. Elena, whom the scarlet chair belonged to, had a very simple grave. Clarisse translated the inscription on her headstone.

"Sometimes we may think that the departure of a loved one is a great injustice, but we are comforted to know that God is right there watching us and gives us comfort," she said in a soft tone. "Elena died broken-hearted."

Harry was careful about his next words as he could feel her sorrow. "I was going to ask about her life, but you don't need to say anything. You may not like talking about it."

"It's OK; it's a well-known story in our family." She paused and took a sip of water from her bottle. "Elena died from a broken heart because her husband was always unfaithful to her—disappearing for days on end while flirting with women outside of the town during his escapades."

"That's such a tragic story—was it one lady in every town?"

"Yes, he was a very handsome man with a charming personality that made him irresistible to women."

"I see ..." Harry did not know what to say next.

"She would spend days waiting for him—sitting in the scarlet chair while crying in shame, feeling heartbroken."

"She still loved him?"

"Yes, despite his infidelity. She still loved him and remained faithful until her death."

"That is a sad ending, and I can imagine her pain," Harry said.

"My mother told me that she could hear her praying at night, asking God for forgiveness—questioning why her marriage was cursed."

"The chair has a strong connection to your family. I can see how the superstition evolved."

"To my mother, it's not a superstition—but an energy that still lingers on, one that has not departed." Clarisse pointed to another grave and suggested they move on before it got dark. It had been a long day for both of them.

He lay the remaining flowers in his basket on an unknown grave while making their way to the entrance.

The main entrance was overcrowded with a long queue. Everyone was trying to get home for dinner at the same time. They were dodging graves and headstones along the way out until Clarisse slipped and fell onto a marble gravestone, knocking her knee.

"Ouch!" Clarisse moaned. She had bruised her knee and was in pain.

"Let me help you up," Harry said, lifting her arm onto his shoulder. "Try to balance on the other leg so we can walk out of here."

He held her tightly as they made their way out through the gates and onto a wooden bench.

"Looks like a small lump on your knee and some swelling," Harry said.

"Could have been worse and at least we are out of there." Clarisse grasped his shoulder again and said, "Let's stroll back to the house."

Harry didn't mind the intimacy of holding Clarisse on the way home. The fall had brought them closer together in an unexpected way. Sometimes, things happen out of the blue, and circumstances pave the way for a special moment in time. He held her tightly as she limped back home—making sure she did not put too much pressure on her swollen knee. When they arrived at the house, Harry got some ice from the freezer and made an icepack by wrapping a tea towel around it.

"Here, put this icepack on your knee and ice it every hour to reduce the swelling."

"You know first aid?" Clarisse said.

"Oh yes, part of my job—but also because I do lots of exercises, so it's handy to have."

"It's getting cold now."

"Oh yes, when it gets too cold, take off the ice pack, wait a while and reapply it."

"I see. Thanks, Harry."

Harry wanted to make sure her knee was treated, so he decided to check in at the local hotel that evening rather than return to Manila. Clarisse invited him for lunch with her mother the next day—and as is customary, she reminded Harry that relatives might come and go to check on him.

He wasn't fussed and loved the attention—he was starting to enjoy the company of Clarisse and felt in touch with her. Her presence gave him peace, solace and comfort. She had a calming disposition and was patient towards him. Harry was starting to believe that a relationship could be possible again with the right person. And the thought that he had to travel nine hours by plane to another country to find the perfect girl dumbfounded him. He didn't want to be too philosophical about it, preferring to keep it simple by relishing the moment.

While settling in his hotel room, Harry treated himself to room service and a local rice dish. He took a seat on the balcony facing the hustle and bustle of the main street and looked on. There was enough time to call Matt due to the time difference. He promised he would call him occasionally to let him know how things were going, but also to pick his brains on cultural differences he was experiencing. He had already made a mistake by asking

Clarisse to meet him at the hotel and did not want to repeat that.

"Hi, Matt, how has your day been?"

"I was going to ask you the same question. It's been busy at work and I'm glad to be home. How is everything going for you in Manila?"

"It's been great, and Clarisse is a special girl."

"I'm glad things are working out for you, mate."

"I do want to ask you something though?"

"Yeah. Tell me …"

"It's about this superstition—there is a scarlet chair that keeps popping up in conversation. Sometimes I get the feeling there is more to it."

"You mean they take it seriously, perhaps too seriously?"

"Yeah, something like that."

"Well, that's normal. Their culture is full of superstition—sometimes I think they can't live without it."

"Maybe I'm not used to it and making too much of it?" Harry said philosophically.

"I would not read too much into it, mate. Just go with the flow and try not to be too curious."

"You're probably right. I don't travel much as you do, and I don't have your experience."

"Every family has a superstition, and some are bigger than others—in some families they last for generations," Matt said.

"Must be my curious mind."

"Yeah, you always overthink things. Be a little looser and soak it all in. You're going to find some of their ways weird—but they probably think we do some weird things also," Matt said with a cheeky laugh.

Although Harry could not see Matt in person, he could visualise the expression on his face.

"I think I've got it—hang loose and soak it all in."

"That's the way to do it!"

Harry wished him a good night and took a deep breath, then sipped on his beer.

Maybe I'm just putting too much thought into it, he thought.

6 THE SAMPAGUITA

Clarisse and her mother were enjoying a cup of jasmine tea when a bang on the front door filled the room with an intense vibration. They both jolted from the unexpected intrusion while Marlita dropped her teacup on the table, spilling it onto the tiled floor. Before they could get up to clean the mess, another heavy knock on the door resonated throughout the house. Bang, bang, bang—this time it was louder.

"Open the door, Clarisse, open it now!"

"Who is it?" she yelled from across the room.

"What do you mean, who is it? It's me."

It was her ex-fiancé, and he was angry. Marlita stood opposite the table with frayed nerves; she was shaking.

"I want you to leave right now. You have no business

being here, disturbing my family!" Clarisse said unapologetically. She wanted him out of her life and assumed he had moved on—but he had other plans.

"I heard about that foreigner you brought into the house. So, is this your new lover now?"

"It's none of your business, I don't belong to you anymore, so leave before I call someone."

He banged on the door again—fervently, causing one of the hinges to dislodge. One more thump and the door would collapse.

Marlita ran to the back of the house to call on her sister for help while Clarisse continued persuading him to leave.

"So, who are you going to call? Your relatives, the police; go on, do it—I don't care what you do." He smashed an empty beer bottle on the door sending the glass crashing all over the porch. "Next time I will smash it through your window."

"I'm warning you to leave right now," she said authoritatively.

"Or what? What will you do?"

Clarisse reached for a long, sharp butcher's knife from the kitchen. She was prepared to use it if it meant protecting herself.

"Open the door right now, or I will smash the lock!"

he said desperately.

Clarisse and her mother had experienced his uncontrollable fits of rage before—it usually happened after he had been drinking heavily. Everyone was aware of what he was capable of when under the influence of alcohol. No matter how rational Clarisse tried to be with him, it made no difference to his erratic behaviour.

"I have a knife, and I am prepared to use it if you step inside my house—I'm warning you! Leave right now!" Clarisse had been through so much she did not care anymore if this was to be her last stand. She did not want to be controlled by his incessant behaviours ever again.

There was commotion at the back door as her uncle Pablo and two neighbours rushed into the house carrying baseball bats. Outside, close family friends from the street started to congregate around her ex-fiancé; he was surrounded with nowhere to run. He was warned not to return to the house by the family, or there would be consequences. He had a reputation for bad behaviour that disgraced the whole community. They were not going to succumb to his threats anymore.

He realised he was outnumbered and did not stand a chance. He walked back slowly to his motorbike with his hands in the air. A group of people followed him, waving their bats and screaming obscenities. They wanted to get even while he was disorientated and under the influence of alcohol. A group of neighbours surrounded him and took turns pushing him around until one of them punched him in the nose. He hobbled off to his motorbike with his nose bleeding, jaded by the unexpected attack. He was always cocky, testing everyone around him by driving fear through the residents in the streets. In the past, people were afraid to stop him, but not now. His past infidelities and indiscretions resonated within the community. They had strength in numbers. Individually he was hard to challenge, but as a group, he'd never stand a chance.

The tide had turned on him, and his last attempt to intimidate people was over. He got on his bike while placing a handkerchief on his broken nose and took off in a crazed manner—almost running over a dog in his path.

Clarisse and her mother came running to the front of the house to see him take off like a coward—relieved that it was the last time they would ever see him. They looked at each other and hugged while relatives consoled them. She asked her uncle Pablo if he could repair the hinge on the front door and replace the screws that had snapped. She didn't want Harry to see what had happened—he was an intuitive person and would have sensed something astray. After the commotion, everyone went back to their own business while Clarisse and Marlita contemplated what happened.

"Should I report him to the police, Mother?" Clarisse asked.

"Not for now, my dear, I think he's gone for good. We won't see him again."

"But he still lives in the next suburb; what if he confronts us in the street?"

"Let's see, my dear. If he confronts us again, I will go to the police and get a restraining order against him."

"OK, Mother, let's see." Clarisse was not convinced because she was aware of his potential.

They decided to focus all their energies on repairing the door. Her uncle Pablo arrived with all his tools and started fixing the hinges that had snapped off the wall. The door was balanced precariously and it was surprising it had not fallen completely during the ordeal.

Harry woke up the following day, unaware of what took place at Clarisse's house the previous evening. He had no idea that her ex-fiancé had taken exception to his presence.

The ceiling fan had been working overtime to provide some relief from the heat. He removed the white sheets, stepped out of bed and walked barefoot into the bathroom. The sunlight found its way through the gaps in the bamboo blinds, creating a tapestry of light on the wall. A jasmine fragrance filled the room creating an essence of calm. He felt pleasant, relaxed and finally in touch with himself.

His grey boxer shorts and cotton shirt offered him the comfort appropriate for the warmer climate. Harry walked over to the sink to admire the sampaguita floating in a glass bowl of water. He appreciated the flower more so since his experience in Clarisse's garden. It was customary for hotels to place the sampaguita in the rooms to welcome their guests. For some travellers it was just a flower—but for Harry, it carried a different meaning.

He turned the tap and it made a screeching sound; he had to turn it more than usual to get the water flowing. It had seen better days but was still functional considering its vintage. He put his hands together and splattered water all over his face. He wiped his face clean with the hand towel and looked straight in the mirror. The anxiety of his vision that had once tormented him had gone. He could look at himself and not feel pitiful. He had been through a painful divorce that made him lose confidence in himself. He had seen the ugly side of life and did not want to go back to it again. If it did not turn out as expected with Clarisse, he could always state that the experience had changed him.

The art-deco clock on the wall seemed out of place amongst the nineties-style furniture, but it was functional. He realised he had slept in and he did not have much time to prepare himself before Clarisse's arrival. He had forty-five minutes to get ready; it needed to be quick. There was a possibility she may come late to test him, but that idea soon faded.

Somehow, Harry managed to prepare himself right on cue and dashed downstairs to the foyer. Clarisse had surprised him and was sitting patiently on the sofa.

"Hi, Clarisse, you're on time today," he said.

"I think you passed the initial test so no need to do another."

They both laughed, greeted each other with a kiss on the cheek. She was wearing a sampaguita in her hair to augment the shoulder-length flowing soft curls. Harry couldn't help noticing other men peering at her slender body. She wore a tight white dress with Picasso-style prints of green-and-lime tropical flowers.

"I like the sampaguita in your hair—is that from your mother's garden?"

"Yes, I picked the best one, but it also had to be the right size."

"They had the same flower in my bathroom in a small

bowl of water."

"They do that for the natural jasmine fragrance. Could you smell the flower from a distance?" Clarisse said.

"Oh yes. I could smell the fragrance—it filled the room."

"You look different today than when we first met," Clarisse said.

"Really? Come to think about it—I feel different than when I first arrived."

"You look calmer, relaxed and less tense." She looked at Harry and smiled.

"I suppose we better get going to your house then?"

"Sure. Follow me, and I will show the way." Harry opened the door for her like a perfect gentleman—leading into the bustling main street. Motorbikes, vans and bicycles were everywhere, trying to get ahead of each other by navigating every spare inch of the road.

"How is your swollen knee? You seem to be walking well," he asked.

"I can walk fine now—but it's still tender if you apply pressure. My mother massaged it yesterday and applied a special ointment we use for sprains made from a local herb."

"Does the herb work most of the time?"

"Yes, Harry, as you can see, I'm walking better than

yesterday."

"It was creepy watching you fall over a grave in the cemetery."

"You're not superstitious?" Clarisse smiled and clasped onto Harry's arm. "You don't want people to think we are just strangers … do you?"

"It's fine by me, Clarisse, hold on tightly in case you fall on the pavement," Harry said with a cheeky grin.

"Let's cross the road here."

"The traffic is gridlocked … do you think it's a good idea?" He had never experienced traffic chaos like this before and was feeling unsure about navigating across the road.

"Follow me, I will get you across this crazy road. Make sure you hold on to me though."

Clarisse skilfully led him through the utter madness of the congested road dodging motorbikes with sidecars, taxis and vans. Harry was not sure they'd make it across alive; in a couple of instances he was so close to motorbikes, he thought the worst, that he'd become a road casualty. But he trusted her judgement to get them across the road in one piece.

For the locals, navigating these roads was choreographed madness—there was a balance to it that drivers learned to dodge pedestrians while performing manoeuvres. After they finally made it to the other side of the road it was only a couple of blocks walking distance to her home. Clarisse led the way through the narrow back streets.

Upon arriving at her home, Harry noticed the damage on the front door. "What happened to the door?" he asked inquisitively.

"Oh, nothing, one of the hinges came loose—my uncle Pablo is repairing it. We need to use the back entrance for now."

"Has the door been damaged?" he asked.

Clarisse changed the subject to avoid further questions and pointed towards the back door. "We need to go through this pathway to get to the back door." Grasping Harry by the shoulder, she tugged him towards the back entrance. He was still holding her gently to maintain her balance from her bruised knee.

As they got closer to the back of the house Harry could smell the jasmine fragrance of the sampaguita coming from the back garden. It made him feel serene and comfortable, knowing that the flower symbolised love.

Entering the house through the back door was not the family's preference as it was adjacent to the room with the scarlet chair. All the foot traffic of visitors coming in and out would upset the energy residing in the room.

"Look at all the flowers on the scarlet chair and the petals on the floor," Harry said.

"Oh. That's my mother—she does that every year during the Day of the Dead."

"Does it mean anything?"

"She does it to please the souls of our relatives that have passed away. The jasmine fragrance calms them."

"And the chair?"

"It balances the energy flow from the chair and the environment around it."

"I see. Do you believe all of this?" He was still not sure about the superstition and why it emphasised so much to her family.

"I suppose in a way I do—because I grew up with this superstition as a child."

He wanted to tell Clarisse it was all fictitious and that people don't need to succumb to these superstitions. But he realised this was not his culture, nor his place to question. Clarisse's beliefs belonged to her family, and no matter what he thought about them, it was not going to change their conviction.

"Looks like lunch is ready and there is so much to eat," Clarisse said.

"It does smell wonderful and it is making me hungry," Harry said, holding on to his stomach.

Inside the dining room was a large table with a variety of local cuisine, much of which Harry had never experienced before, except the rice.

Clarisse got him a plate and one by one explained every dish on the table. "I think you would like to try this one with the crispy pork and rice."

"Just looking at it is making me hungry." Harry gulped.

"I won't say where the pork came from," Clarisse said.

"Let me guess … the piggery at the back of the house?"

"Yes, and my uncle Pablo has spent all day preparing it."

They filled their plates with food and made their way to the table to feast on the delicious recipes. While they took their seats, Marlita appeared from nowhere and without warning. She placed another dish on the table. It was the first time she had the opportunity to speak to Harry without distractions.

"So, we get to meet properly this time?" Marlita said.

"Hello, Ms Garcia. It's a pleasure to meet you again." Her abrupt introduction did not bother Harry.

"You have come a long way to spend time with my daughter. Don't you have good girls in Australia?"

He did not know what to say without being

confrontational. "I'm sure there are good girls in Australia, but I have not met any of them yet."

"How did you meet Clarisse? Did Marjorie have something to do with it?"

"It's very complicated, but I first found out about Clarisse through an introduction from my best friend. He had already been to Manila to see a girl called Alicia and returned home."

"I thought as much," Marlita said sarcastically.

Clarisse was feeling embarrassed by the line of questioning her mother had taken and reminded her that Harry was a guest in the house.

"So, Harry, my daughter has been through a lot, and I don't want her to get hurt again. I'm sure we understand each other?" Marlita took her seat at the table and looked directly at him with piercing eyes—ignoring her daughter's previous request to be polite.

"I have no intention of hurting anyone, Ms Garcia, especially Clarisse. She is a beautiful person—I am fortunate to be able to spend time with her in the short time that I'm here."

Marlita was not convinced—she had heard it all before. For Marlita, he was just like the others—the only difference being he was stupid enough to spend all his money to travel to Manila to win over her daughter's heart.

"The chair can sense your presence—I know it, and I don't think it's happy," Marlita said.

An argument then broke out between Clarisse and her mother in their local language. It appeared by their body language that Clarisse asked her mother not to be so hard on Harry and to calm down.

"I'm sorry about her behaviour, Harry. I wasn't expecting it."

Harry turned towards Clarisse with a mannered grin. "I'm not here to marry your mother—although I want to maintain a good relationship with her." He took her hand and gently caressed it. "I am a foreigner, and it's going to raise several questions about my integrity. I don't know your customs—I can't speak your language. I'm at a disadvantage from the beginning."

"I guess you're right, but she could still be polite—you don't have to like someone to be nice to them."

"It's OK. I'm not offended. Maybe next time, as she gets to know me better, she will be more understanding."

"I guess so … maybe next time." Clarisse nodded and took a couple of deep breaths. It was her way of calming her delicate nerves.

"Where has your mother gone now?" Harry asked.

"When she is angry, she goes to the room with the

scarlet chair and talks to her dead relatives. She prays to them—sometimes up to an hour."

"She prays to the people in the picture frames?"

"Yes … and sometimes she prays to bless our family." Clarisse took a deep breath. "The room is like our family altar—we have a cross and rosary beads next to the picture frames."

"Does she sit in the scarlet chair while praying?"

"No one is allowed to sit in the chair; Mother told me when I was a child that the negative energy could sense your presence—it can make the chair unhappy."

"I remember you telling me during our first dinner together that the chair belonged to your great-grandmother, Elena, who died of a broken heart."

"Yes, the sadness stayed with our family." She took a spoon and passed it to Harry. "Let's eat before the relatives start walking in one by one to check you out."

"Oh yes, you warned me about that."

"And don't worry, they are not like my mother. They are looking forward to meeting you."

"Is your aunty from the hotel here also?"

"Yes, how could you forget her?"

The lunch parade went well, and Harry got a taste of the culture—food, people, music and celebrity status as relatives came to greet him and then move on to the next house. It was like a procession starting from one home at the beginning of the street and ending at the last residence. There were no invitations or any formality involved—everyone was free to go house to house at their discretion.

Clarisse's house brought the most attention as news had spread that Harry the foreigner was in town. His easy-going nature and personality pleased them because they could have a conversation without feeling embarrassed. The level of English with most of her relatives was surprisingly good; they had no issue conversing with him. Most of the talk was about his home country, but some questioned him about his intentions in a roundabout way.

Clarisse warned him about her aunties and how they would be probing. Clarisse was the most beautiful girl in the town and their Aphrodite, the goddess of love. She was popular not just because of her looks—she was a genuine and caring person that had been unlucky in love, and they all felt she deserved better.

One thing Harry noticed was the room with the scarlet chair was closed. It was unofficially out of bounds—her relatives never mentioned it in conversation and it only added to the mystery. If things did not make sense, he wanted to work it out—find the solution or unravel the mystery. That is why Harry enjoyed fixing old collectable cars because they required problem-solving and finding unorthodox ways of repairing.

"I think that was the last family to visit us," Clarisse said.

"It's been a long day, and it was great to meet all your family and relatives. Your aunty I met at the hotel—she has an incredible personality."

"She has always been the bubbly one—everyone loves her." She poured a cup of tea in her glass and added milk and two teaspoons of sugar. "I enjoyed being around her when I was younger—she always made me feel important," Clarisse said.

"I got a sense of that also. She has a wicked sense of humour."

"Do you want some tea before leaving for the hotel?" Clarisse asked with a teapot in hand.

"Yes, I could do with a tea after all that." He was feeling tired and mentally exhausted from all the attention.

"My uncle Pablo has offered to take us on his motorbike and the sidecar to your hotel."

"I have never been in a sidecar before. Is it safe?" Harry was feeling apprehensive.

"Hold on tight, you will be fine; if it gets too much,

close your eyes," Clarisse said.

Harry gulped and smiled. "I'm sure I will get there in one piece."

As they started walking to the back entrance and into the sampaguita garden they passed the room with the scarlet chair. Harry couldn't let go of his interest in the mystique that surrounded the superstition. He also pondered about the tragedy that preceded it. As they walked past the room, there was a knock on the door and a screeching sound. It resembled someone moving furniture although there was nobody in the room.

"Did you hear that?" Harry said.

"Oh, that's the wind hitting against the door … maybe a picture frame has fallen."

Harry was bemused because there were no windows in the room. "Should we check and fix the frame?"

"No need to go in there—my mother can take care of it. She will be back soon," Clarisse said hesitantly.

There was another screech coming from the room. "Are you sure there is no one in there moving things around?"

"It's nothing, Harry. Let's go, my uncle Pablo is waiting." Clarisse took hold of his arm and gently tugged it in the direction of the garden. "Come on—my uncle Pablo is waiting for us."

There was a jasmine smell coming from the room—he assumed it was the jasmine that decorated the scarlet chair. The fragrance was not fresh—it had become stagnant with a rotting undertone that pierced the nostrils.

It was too early for the flowers to start rotting … they were picked fresh from the garden yesterday, he thought.

From the time he arrived at Clarisse's home, there was a constant reminder that the superstition was alive and well. There was no denying that something unusual was going on. The scarlet chair was not only an antique piece of furniture held in remembrance of her great-grandmother—it was more than that. There were too many events that did not make sense. To make matters worse, nobody wanted to talk about the chair— which only added to the mystery.

They put on their bike helmets and stepped into the sidecar. It was a restricted space and Harry had to cuddle next to Clarisse. He didn't mind, and it was the first time they had been so close.

"Hold on to me if it gets too much," Clarisse said. She knew he was in for a rough ride.

The motorbike took off—the rattle of the sidecar was imposing. Clarisse assured him it was OK and that the equipment was maintained. Her uncle Pablo dodged other motorbikes in a choreography of movement that only locals knew how to dance. It was utter controlled chaos; everyone understood how to navigate the congestion. "Fight for every inch of the road without being too aggressive" was the mantra. There were a couple of sharp twists and turns that required Harry to hold on to Clarisse. He didn't mind and was loving it.

There was no doubt Clarisse's uncle Pablo was a great driver—he was able to get them to the hotel promptly, beating all other modes of transport.

They both removed their helmets upon arrival to refresh themselves from the stifling heat. Clarisse's hair waved in the warm breeze as she tied it to stop it flying around. Her crimson-coloured lipstick and dash of dark blue eyeliner accentuated her almond-shaped eyes. All Harry could do at that moment was stare and say nothing; he was in a daze, reflecting on her immense beauty. In his eyes, she was a picture of perfection and everything he expected in a girl. He was starting to have feelings for Clarisse and was unhappy that he was leaving. Tomorrow was his last day in Manila—he was conscious of leaving her behind.

They stood at the front entrance of the hotel like solitary figures while her uncle Pablo waited to take Clarisse home.

"So, you're going back to Manila tomorrow morning?" Clarisse said.

Harry folded his arms and nodded. "Yes. My flight is departing at 9:30 p.m. How about you?"

"I need to go back to Manila and prepare for work the day after you leave."

"I guess you're taking the same bus back home also?"

"No, I can't, Harry. I need to stay with my mother for another day."

"Oh, I understand." Harry's tone dropped a few decibels.

"Well … I wanted to ask what time you were planning on leaving? The buses run every hour and I could take you to the bus terminal."

"Could you do that?" Harry's face lit up with a brilliant smile.

"Of course, I can take you there. I will get my uncle Pablo to take us in the sidecar again." She got close to Harry and whispered, "I think he likes you—otherwise, he would have left by now."

"The only person I need to win over is your mother."

"Don't hold your breath with her," Clarisse said. "Anyway, because you're new to this place I don't want you catching the wrong bus—it's a busy terminal."

"I couldn't agree more. When we arrived a couple of

days ago, I was so confused. If you hadn't been with me, I would have lost myself amongst the crowd of people."

"So, what time should we pick you up?"

"Does 9 a.m. suit?" Harry asked.

"Yeah, I will meet you here at the front at nine."

"Oh, Clarisse, you need to be on time … and no tests, OK?"

Clarisse nodded. "OK then. Have a good night and see you tomorrow."

Clarisse instinctively put her arms around Harry and hugged him for a couple of seconds. She was happy to be with him, but also sad he was leaving.

For his part, Harry was also feeling an emptiness. He felt his stomach muscles tighten as he let go of her.

"Goodbye, and I will see you tomorrow."

He waved to Clarisse as she hopped into the sidecar and put on her helmet. She waved back to him frequently—smiling and pointing at her watch.

Harry went along with the joke and threw both hands up in the air and said, "Not again!"

7 THE LOVE PREMONITION

Clarisse arrived home and in time for afternoon tea in the garden with Marjorie, who was leaving that evening by bus. Clarisse had wanted to catch up with her beforehand and discuss some ideas with Marjorie—something significant that required her support. They had known each other since they were young children and worked in the same company. There were no secrets between them—they shared their most personal feelings. They lived next door to each other in Manila and were always at hand to support one another.

"Marjorie, I want to ask you for a special favour—but you mustn't speak to anyone about this." Marjorie adjusted her seat and looked directly at Clarisse. She had her full attention.

"Well … what is it?"

"I have feelings for Harry and he's leaving tomorrow." She took a sip of the tea and held on to her cup. "I know he feels the same way about me."

"I had a sense you two were going well. So, what is it?"

"I'm going to use the scarlet chair for Harry."

Marjorie spat out her tea and looked at her crossly. "You're *what*? Haven't you forgotten what happened to you three months ago—want me to remind you?"

"I understand it makes you angry. Can you listen to me for one moment?" They both paused and looked at each other.

"OK … explain," Marjorie said.

"You know the power of the chair and how it can predict the outcome of relationships?"

"I also know that it can hurt you, Clarisse, and I don't want you to go through it again."

"You remember the rules of the superstition?"

"Yes, the scarlet chair won't hurt you if the prophecy contains true love and desire."

"Yes, correct—that is because the chair feeds on negative energy in a relationship that has gone sour—infidelity, cheating, lies, adultery and abuse." Clarisse took a deep breath to relax her nerves.

"You want to prophesise the relationship with Harry

on the scarlet chair—after being together only five days?"

"Yes." Clarisse was steadfast in her conviction.

"I don't know, Clarisse. Maybe you're asking for too much this time." Marjorie lifted the teapot and poured another cup of tea. "You can do this later on, when you've gotten to know each other better."

"I understand, Marjorie, but think about it … what is going to change between now and then? He will go back to his country; we'll chat over the internet … and then what? How much effort are we supposed to put into a long-distance relationship? And then if I am lucky, he may visit me once every three months. How is that supposed to work?"

"I understand what you are saying. I agree in principle—but I don't want to be responsible for knowing that this could put you back in the hospital," Marjorie said assertively.

"The chair can't hurt me because there is true love and desire. All it does is feed on the negative energy of illicit relationships, sucking it out through your body— draining you of all passion for life. The chair has no choice but to provide me with a warning about my future relationship with Harry. I promise … I will be fine."

"I don't know, Clarisse."

"Please … I need your help." She put her hand over

her face and tilted her head down. The conversation was not going as planned.

Marjorie paused for a while and was in deep thought. "I know that if I don't help, you will do it anyway—you're stubborn. So, I may as well be there just in case you get into trouble."

Clarisse stood motionless and they did not talk for a few minutes. They sipped on cold lemon tea while a gentle breeze lifted the fragrance of jasmine from the sampaguita into the air. It calmed them down and made the surroundings serene.

She stared at Marjorie with a level of intensity—her eyebrows lifted and forehead wrinkled.

"The plan is to monitor my mother and keep her busy while I go into the room with the scarlet chair."

"That is fine … but what are you going to do in there … what is the plan?" Marjorie said hesitantly.

"I will do what I have always done—sit in the chair and share my convictions."

"Something I always wanted to ask is about the energy—is it good or bad? I have never understood it."

She took Marjorie's hand and held it, rubbing it gently. "It's not evil energy but a sad one that has become lost in a world of anguish and sadness. It feeds itself with self-importance by destroying relationships that have become sour, toxic and broken down due to infidelity, cheating and unfaithfulness."

"Are you telling me it thinks it's helping you?" Marjorie asked.

"Well, yes. However, it does not understand its strength or when to stop, because it lacks a conscience."

"And that's why you get hurt … I mean, mentally."

"It drains all your mental strength and emotion, so you become immobilised. If it becomes too powerful, it can drain your conscience."

Marjorie was intrigued—it was the first time Clarisse ever shared her experience with the chair. It was forbidden to discuss the scarlet chair, and her mother made sure of it—always cutting down any conversation about it prematurely.

"How about we meet around dinnertime when my mother is in the kitchen cooking?"

"OK, Clarisse, I hope you have got this right, and know what you're doing … I will see you then."

They finished their tea and went their separate ways. Clarisse went to have a late afternoon nap before initiating her plan with Marjorie. It was a calculated, high-risk move she was taking, considering the effect it had had on her before. She believed to have found the loophole and the source of anger within the energy. If she were right, she would be able to neutralise the effect of the negative energy while at the same time find out about her future with Harry. The scarlet chair was a vehicle—an embodiment of the power Elena left behind. Pieces of her broken heart remained in the chair. It was the last place she touched in the physical world before passing on after her death.

Is this what happens when you die broken-hearted? A part of you stays behind in retribution of the burning pain and suffering endured while living your life of sorrow? Somehow, Clarisse had worked out the chair's source of frustration and how to manage it. In this case, use it to her advantage, and if she could, vindicate her previous experience. It required bravery and stubbornness—both of which aptly described her personality.

Clarisse was in the dining room with her mother preparing dinner. It was a traditional recipe—an appealing crackling pork dish, marinated in vinegar, soy sauce, garlic, black peppercorns, and browned in oil. If you were not hungry, you'd become so. The aroma filled the room and triggered your appetite like an aperitif— making you succumb to the delicacy and ask for more. Towards the end of the meal, Marjorie arrived as planned and nodded to her in acknowledgement. Clarisse excused herself from the table and told her mother she was going to clean up, while Marjorie remained behind keeping her mother company. Marlita had a soft spot for Marjorie; they could talk for hours, making it the perfect decoy.

Clarisse quietly walked to the backroom, taking small steps and wearing no slippers—she did not want to make a sound. She slowly turned the doorknob, realising it had a couple of clicks in it due to its age. One click, two clicks and then another until the doorknob turned ninety degrees and the door was ajar. There was an eerie freshness in the air and it was odd considering the room had no windows and it was a humid evening. It was not the first time Clarisse had experienced an unusual change in room temperature.

Clarisse looked around the room anxiously—the picture frames, the console table and petals from the jasmine sambac covered the floor. They had not been removed from the Day of the Dead as it would have angered the spirits. The side lamp was always on, twenty-four hours a day—moderating the dark ambience that suffocated the space in the room. The candles lit in memory of the dead were melting. The wax had penetrated onto the dark-red mahogany console table, leaving white stains.

Clarisse stood motionless, looking at the chair to exert

her authority. The chair sensed fear in the hearts of young women and fed on their grief. She adjusted her body to sit upright in the chair while an unusual scraping sound came from the ornately carved legs below. It was the same sound that Harry had talked about, and she had avoided it in conversation many times. Leaning into the chair and with her feet firmly planted, she began the process for extracting a vision.

Triggering a premonition required an understanding of what angered the chair and Clarisse was fully aware of how to set it off. Envisioning herself with Harry by sharing precious moments that accentuated the feelings of true love was enough to wake the negative energy. To start with, she imagined holding hands with Harry and walking together in a luscious green tropical garden— never too sensual as the chair detested sexual innuendos and tendencies. As her visions grew stronger, the chair felt provoked, causing it to become infuriated.

A discharge of negative energy followed—mimicking the cold hands of a dead person and holding her down by the torso. Clarisse could feel the pressure of the cold hands mounting, but she was unperturbed. The left hand had a ring on the index finger that she recognised as having belonged to Elena. She tried to push the hands away, but they were too strong, thrusting her back each time. She was being held down like a psychiatric patient strapped down with a leather belt. The sense of not being able to move her body freely caused her to become anxious—but she held her emotions together and was not going to panic.

The chair was fighting back and was annoyed about Clarisse's inner strength and resistance. It made more screeching sounds, although it did not rattle or move from its position on the floor. It was a peculiar set of circumstances that did not make sense—someone was making those sounds in the room, and she could not see where it was coming from. The intensity of the energy grew, and the pressure on her torso mounted while the screeching became louder and more frequent. The chair was awake, and its ferocity increased every minute.

The picture frames holding the souls of her dead relatives fell flat on the console table, one by one, sequentially. They were not happy—the energy used them to incite more fear into her. Clarisse kept focusing on her visions of togetherness with Harry despite attempts by the chair to thwart her. She had been through this twice before—having learned the survival techniques from her previous experience. Although her last attempt had made her sick to the point that she ended up in a hospital, she had also learned about the chair's vulnerabilities and how to challenge it.

Like anything in life, the energy was not perfect. If you looked hard enough amongst the shrouded fear, it had weaknesses that could be exploited. The first rule was not to panic and stay focused on your beliefs as the chair preyed on weak hearts and minds. The chair was tactful and sought your submission by feeding you with fear and torment. Not physical pain but an affliction of the brain. It would turn the screw and increase the intensity until you eventually let go and succumbed—and every negative conception about love and desire would feed its desperate innuendos. It's how the energy survived all this time, on the misery of relationships gone wrong: infidelity, adultery, cheating, lies. Where love had transgressed into hate and anguish.

The scarlet chair was not getting its way and it was finding it challenging to control Clarisse. It increased its ferocity again—the screeching got louder, the stench from the rotting flowers became putrid, the chair started to rattle profusely. The energy of the hands holding her down was growing stronger with mounting pressure. And while all this was taking place, her mother's rosary beads lying next to the wooden cross became dislodged and flew across the room.

The chair was having a tantrum and going to great

lengths to make her apprehensive and uneasy. It remembered Clarisse from last time—realising it was only a matter of time until it could break her mind and feed off her memories. But it had misjudged her this time—she was doing this for unconditional love. She had twice the strength and wisdom as before and would see it through no matter what challenges the chair threw at her.

"Give me the premonition," she said while biting her lip and clenching her delicate hands. "Give it to me now!"

A sharp ray of amber light filtering through a crack in the tin roof above her pointed onto her face like a laser beam. It blinded her view for a split second before moving slowly in a constant motion onto the console table and onto the altar with the picture frames of her dead relatives. There, the light remained motionless for ten seconds until it vanished into the dark haze of the room. The energy had passed over and had given up. The scarlet chair stood still as quiet descended into the room—no more screeching and rattling. The foul stench had made way for a new jasmine freshness in the air.

Clarisse was free to move around, and the cold hands that held her down had tucked themselves away into a pocket of frailty. She did not rush out of the chair in a panic; instead, she shifted in it to make herself comfortable while gazing at the altar. There was peace in the room—the cold air transformed into a moderate warmth.

Marlita came rushing in with Marjorie beside her—they had heard a commotion from the kitchen and feared Clarisse could be in danger again.

"What have you done this time, my precious? How many times have I warned you about sitting in the chair?"

"Mother, it's fine, and I am OK this time."

She gripped Clarisse's arm—holding her close, they hugged with fervour. "Why do it this time? There was no reason to go back to the chair."

"But Mother, you have missed the whole point because of your superstitious fear." Clarisse had tears in her eyes as she silently confronted her mother.

"What do you mean, my dear? I am only protecting you."

"Yes, and in the process, you allowed the chair to control us—our lives, our feelings and who we could love."

"You did this for Harry, didn't you? I am not stupid, Clarisse, and I know why you're here."

"I saw the premonition—I know about our future together."

She caressed Clarisse on the forehead, gently combing her fingers through her hair.

"The only way to force a premonition from the chair without hurting oneself is to hold memories of pure love. The energy could not break down your feelings for him—unable to feed on such a memory. In return, it had to give a warning so it could save itself," Marlita said.

"So, the energy is gone, Mother?"

"No, not gone. It's beaten for now … its power diluted. It does not have the same strength as before." She was holding her rosary around her right hand and close to her lips. She kissed it and thanked God that Clarisse was not affected by the negative energy of the scarlet chair.

Marlita could not help noticing the petals from the jasmine sambac lying on the floor, looking fresh—as though they had been plucked from her cultured garden only moments ago. The jasmine fragrance filled the room with tranquillity. It was a serene feeling that had always evaded this dreary room.

Even though the room had no windows, layers of filtered light manage to force their way through cracks in the tin roof.

"Come, let's take you back to your room," Marlita said.

Marjorie helped support Clarisse, slowly making their way to her bedroom at a steady pace. While on the chair, the ghostly hands messed up her hair and stretched her tight-fitted shorts that accentuated her thin legs. Her fitted shirt was torn to one side and her buttons were missing.

"Not a word to anyone about this ... both of you need to keep this quiet." Marlita was concerned about the superstition becoming the talk of the town. It had happened before—the last thing she wanted was another careless girl trying her luck on the scarlet chair in the name of love.

They both nodded in silence. Marlita could see that Clarisse had been sapped of her strength and was tired.

Marlita was concerned about the fragility of younger women when clinging on to love in hope. It made them devoid of any common sense—realising this in her daughter.

When they are desperate in love and emotions are running high, the negative energy of the scarlet chair becomes a risk worth taking.

The scarlet chair will offer a warning of something that is going to happen, but at a price: that toll is your mind, it saps all emotions and fears to feed itself. It will try and render you hapless if you fight back.

The scarlet chair was a guarded secret in the family for those reasons. No one outside their immediate family was aware of its powers. Marlita's concern was that Clarisse had shared this secret with Marjorie. Even though Marjorie had heard about the superstition like everyone else when she was growing up, today she witnessed the power of the scarlet chair for the first time—she knew what it could do.

How could she stop Marjorie using the scarlet chair if she was unlucky in love? It was a problem the family didn't need right now.

Clarisse has settled down for the night and fell asleep with her mother by her bedside. As for the room with the scarlet chair—it looked like every other room in the house—a warm and cosy place where everyone was welcome. The question was, how long that would last?

The previous time the energy returned to the scarlet chair, it was wiser and more intense. It also learned from its experience and how to cunningly leverage thoughts differently to gain an advantage. It mutated like a virus learning how to adapt to every new situation. It could feel the presence of another person in the house when previously it did not have that perception. It had extended its reach beyond the confines of the scarlet chair and become more powerful over the years.

8 ONE MORE DAY

Harry had settled in for the evening, unbeknown to him what had taken place with Clarisse. As far as he was aware, she was catching up on a good night's sleep. She had been vague about the chair and avoided any questions about it. For Harry, it remained a mystery shrouded in secrecy.

He was packing his bag to return to Manila the next day. Clarisse and her uncle Pablo had offered to take him to the bus terminal—they needed to make sure he caught the right bus and didn't end up in the wrong place. He was leaving the next evening for his flight back home to Melbourne. His journey was coming to an end. But it was not the packing that made him feel restless—the prospect he would have to say goodbye to Clarisse is what bothered him the most. He could not stop thinking about her.

Harry had a big decision to make—continue spending more time with Clarisse and give the friendship a chance to grow or leave mid-stream with uncertainty hanging over their romance. How could he leave her not knowing what could have been? It was tormenting him, and time was running out. He understood once he was back home that a long-distance relationship would be challenging to maintain. He did not know the success rate of long-distance romances—but common sense would suggest it had a high failure rate. Sure, you could chat every night and see each other through a webcam, but it was not the same.

The experience was different; you could not pick the flowers or smell the jasmine from the sampaguita—or go for a wild ride in a sidecar down a congested street while holding on to each other for support. They were all subtle things that brought you together. He could not do that six thousand miles away.

Harry decided to send an email to his boss—although they were three hours behind Melbourne, if he acted quickly, he may get a response by the morning. But what would he say to him without lying? Harry had worked in the same company for almost ten years and had known his boss for the same period. He did not want to lie and say he was sick or that there had been a flight cancellation. But how would his boss react to him coming back to work later because of a girl? It was possible that if his boss did not have empathy for his situation he could be reprimanded or dismissed for abandoning his job. Harry was in a pickle and torn by desire.

Damn this, I'm just going to do it. And if they don't like it, then OK, I will find another job, he thought.

Harry connected his laptop to the hotel internet and prepared his email. He explained to his boss the truth about Clarisse and why he wanted to stay an extra two days in Manila. Now all he had to do was sit back and wait for the response by morning. His boss was very efficient and always responded to email messages quickly, even after hours from his iPhone. Writing an email and sending it to his boss was therapeutic for his mind. However, he was still apprehensive about losing his job and the consequences.

Next morning, Harry checked his email to see if his boss had responded—but there was no reply and he would check again later. He was running late and skipped breakfast. He made his way to the front of the hotel in a hurry. He waited for Clarisse and her uncle Pablo to pick him up as arranged with the sidecar. As a man of routine, he had the same breakfast, poached eggs on toast, and sat at the same chair and table at the corner end of the dining area. The waiter already knew what Harry was going to order for breakfast. They would look at each other and nod in agreement, such was their understanding.

Clarisse was on cue, unlike in their second meeting. Harry didn't have to prove himself this time—it would have been unnecessary for Clarisse to make him wait. She waved at Harry in a swiping motion and asked him to jump into the sidecar while her uncle Pablo managed the luggage. She was wearing a crimson dress, tightly fitted and just above her knees. Her hair was tied back in a bun—her lips accentuated with a pale red lipstick. Her trademark extended eyelashes stole the show and made her glitter in the sun each time they blinked.

Clarisse hugged onto his arm and sat close to him in the restricted space of the sidecar, smiling as her uncle Pablo mounted the motorbike and put on his helmet. It was going to be another journey through the congested streets leading to the bus terminal. It was only a couple of blocks from the hotel and the quickest way to get there was by cutting through the back streets.

Why is she so happy? I'm leaving today, and she should be sad, he thought.

"I want to say something, Harry." Her voice rose a couple of decibels over the sound coming from the street.

"What is it?"

"I have a surprise."

Harry looked at her intently, waiting. "Are you going to tell me, Clarisse?"

"I'm coming with you to Manila, and my bag is in the carriage. See, look there." She pointed to her blue carry-on bag.

Harry turned his head to check the carriage—the blue carry-on luggage was next to his suitcase. "You are coming back to Manila with me on the bus?"

"Yes."

"No wonder you were smiling before," Harry said.

"You were wondering why I wasn't sad that you were leaving?

"It crossed my mind."

"Ha, ha. I did that on purpose to see your reaction."

"Well, you did a good job." Harry took a deep breath and sighed. He was relieved that Clarisse was coming back with him on the bus.

Harry checked his laptop before leaving his hotel, and he had not received a response from his boss. He would check again from his iPhone once he was on the bus.

As they turned the last corner, the bus station was directly ahead of them—but their joy would soon turn to anguish. A man on a red Honda motorbike had been following them from the hotel and was now driving erratically alongside them. He was holding a baseball bat and waving it around—yelling at Clarisse and demanding her uncle Pablo pull aside. Clarisse was pointing at him and raising her voice. It appeared she knew him.

"Go away and leave us alone!" she said.

"Do you know this guy?" Harry asked as the sidecar swooped side to side to avoid a collision with the motorbike.

"It's my ex-fiancé and he's crazy."

"How did he find us here?"

"It's a small town, Harry—everyone knows where you are staying … he found out." There was a loud clang from the carriageway as the baseball bat connected with the sidecar. Her ex-fiancé was out of control and in a rage.

Uncle Pablo asked if he could stop and confront him. Clarisse waved him on—it would not be the first time her uncle and ex-fiancé were at loggerheads with each other.

"We are nearly at the bus terminal, Uncle Pablo … another hundred metres … keep going!"

There was another clang of the baseball bat on Harry's side—just missing his arm by centimetres. He looked back at him and could see the intense stare of a man gone mad.

"Quick, Uncle Pablo … we are here. Stop at the

entrance!" Clarisse said, pointing towards the two security guards.

It did not perturb her ex-fiancé who continued threatening them and waving his bat around. Clang! It was another strike of the baseball bat next to Clarisse. She instinctively ducked her shoulders hitting the side of her head on the frame of the sidecar.

"Ouch," she sighed clasping her head with her hand.

Harry looked over, concerned, and said, "Are you OK, Clarisse?"

"It's just a bump. I'm fine."

Fortunately, the security guards could see the commotion and acted quickly, dashing towards the sidecar. Her uncle Pablo parked the sidecar as close as he could to the entrance and jumped out—ready to confront her ex. He was in the mood for a good fight and would do anything to protect Clarisse.

Her ex-fiancé lost control of his motorbike as it hit the curb, causing it to roll over and crash to the ground directly in front of them. He tumbled onto the pavement, rolling over several times before landing next to a vending machine. Passengers from the overcrowded bus terminal came rushing over to see the incident. Some of them wanted to help Clarisse who had taken a knock on the side of her head.

Harry stood motionless, coming to grips with what had transpired as he held Clarisse in his arms. He frantically took his handkerchief from his side pocket and covered her wound. It was a small cut and bruise with a trickle of blood. She had avoided serious injury.

"It's fine, Clarisse ... your cut is not that bad, and your uncle Pablo has gone to get help at the bus terminal."

"That crazy bastard ... I'm so sorry to put you through this," Clarisse said with tears sliding down her face.

The security guards apprehended her ex-fiancé—he was lying on the ground and grasping his leg in pain. "Oh, oh," he groaned, grinding his teeth in agony. The fall was severe enough to have injured his right leg, and he was in some discomfort. There was not much the security guards needed to do to apprehend him because he could not move. His spiteful rage had turned foul, and like previously, he came out second best. Perhaps this time he was in enough pain to understand all his attempts to get even with Clarisse were futile. She had absolutely no feelings for him anymore.

She was given first aid and was fit enough to travel back to Manila. Her uncle Pablo said goodbye to both and wished them well. He mounted his motorbike and took off into the clogged traffic.

Clarisse had a small cut and a bruise next to her right eye. Although the swelling made her feel uncomfortable, she was not in a lot of pain. They took their seats on the bus and placed their bags in front of them. They both looked at one another and sighed as they lay back, placing their heads on the headrest. It had been a stressful morning, and they had the jitters from what had transpired.

"I think I might just rest for thirty minutes and have a quick nap," Harry said.

"I think I will join you."

Clarisse placed her head gently onto Harry's shoulders and immediately started to doze off.

For his part, he enjoyed having her close to him. He wanted to put his arms around her but thought it could wait. He didn't want to be seen taking advantage of her even though he had a strong desire to hold her tightly.

Thirty minutes into the bus journey, Harry woke up from his nap. Clarisse was already awake and listening to music on her iPhone. She looked at Harry and removed her earphones.

"How long was I out for?" Harry asked.

"About thirty minutes. How do you feel?"

"Much better; I hope I was not snoring."

"I could hear you from the back of the bus."

"You're kidding me …" Harry sighed.

She smiled and put her hand over her mouth and said, "I was only kidding … you were very quiet."

"Want some water?" Harry asked.

"I will be fine … I already have some here."

Harry shifted in his seat and pulled back the recliner so he could sit upright. "So, how is your head feeling?"

"I am OK, considering what we went through."

"Are you going to tell me more about your ex-fiancé?" He looked her straight in the eye, expecting an explanation.

"There is not a lot to talk about, Harry—other than he was unfaithful, a cheat and lied to me a lot."

"That's not good. And how did you find out about his infidelity?"

Clarisse did not want to mention the scarlet chair and her premonition, but did not want to lie to him either.

"I found out from people at his work that he was fooling around." She was not comfortable talking about her ex-fiancé because she wanted him out of her thoughts.

"I see; well, my story is similar."

"You mean with your ex-wife?"

"Yes, she confessed to having an affair with her boss while travelling for work." He paused for a moment to gather his thoughts. "It was going on for a while—she was always carrying on about her career."

"Did she travel a lot?"

"Almost once a week and it involved overnight stays."

Clarisse took his hand and held it tight. "You trusted her … right?"

"Yes. It never dawned on me what she was doing, and it caught me by surprise." He turned and looked at her with a smirk. "Looks like we were both diddled?"

She looked at Harry with a confused look. "Diddled?"

"Oh, that means cheated, swindled, deceived—those sorts of things."

"Ha, ha. At least I learned a new word today."

Harry connected his phone to the Wi-Fi signal inside the bus and checked his email. His boss had responded.

Hi Harry,

Thanks for getting in touch with us about your holiday overseas. I understand you want to stay a couple more days in Manila. I spoke to our boss, and our advice is to take the extra time off, and we will discuss further when you come back. Get back to us with the return date as soon as possible. In the meantime, enjoy your extended break.

All the best,
Jim

"What are you doing?" Clarisse said.

"I'm cancelling my flight."

"You're what?" She was confused and unsure of what had come over him. "The flight is tonight."

"I have decided to stay for another two days—I'm changing my flights before they charge me a cancellation fee."

Clarisse was ecstatic and put her hands in the air. "Yeah!" she declared, punching the air with her fist.

"Yes, I'm finding the airline's number right now. I will call them."

She was so excited that she hugged him firmly and then kissed him on the cheek. Harry did not want to let go of Clarisse and encouraged her to keep hugging by remaining still. It was as close as they had ever been since they first met—it felt great. It was intimate and not explicit in any way. Harry never understood what took her so long. But in her culture, relationships take time and love is a nurtured process; step by step and bit by bit they slowly fall in love with one another.

Harry now had an extra two days with Clarisse, and he couldn't believe his good fortune. He didn't want his romance to be a fling—boy meets a girl from another country, has a good time and then spends the rest of his life dreaming about what could have been. He wanted to give the relationship every opportunity to grow and not be rushed into anything because of an impending deadline.

Harry had managed to change his flight to one leaving two days later. He incurred a change fee but did not care. It was a small price to pay to stay longer with Clarisse. She was listening in on the phone call with anticipation. She clenched her fist and made the sign of victory when she overheard he had successfully changed his booking. They were both smiling and couldn't wait to plan the next two days together.

The bus was fifteen minutes away from Harry's hotel and had made good time. They decided to have a nap in the afternoon, and Clarisse would return to the hotel restaurant in the evening to have dinner. It dawned on them that it was a dinner they were not supposed to have. It was one of the benefits of Harry changing his flight. For the first time since they met at Manila Airport, they were having dinner together in a reputable restaurant—no chaperones, inhibitions or testing of any sort. They had passed all that—it made them feel great.

Before going to bed, Harry thought of giving Matt a call to talk about his experience today. He had been through so much that he needed someone to talk to. Although he was grateful it was over, the incident with

Clarisse's ex-fiancé had played on his mind.

"Hi Matt, it's me, Harry."

"How are you, mate, and how is Manila going?"

"Very well. Clarisse is the most beautiful person I have ever met."

"Really?"

"And I need to thank you for the introduction. I know I was difficult at first …"

"I have known you a long time, Harry, and know when you need a little push in the right direction."

"Listen, I want to ask something." Harry paused for a moment. "We had an incident today at the bus terminal—her ex-fiancé turned up."

"You're kidding me!"

"Baseball bat and everything. It was like one of those James Bond movies … he chased us on a motorbike while we were going to the bus terminal with her uncle."

"That's so scary … what happened?"

"He crashed his bike and hurt himself just as we arrived at the bus terminal—he nearly hit me on the head with his bat while I was in the sidecar!"

"That's a close call … so he crashed his bike? That will teach him." Matt never minced his words.

"Matt, it was just the whole thing—I wasn't expecting it."

"Sounds like you got rattled, mate."

"Yeah … sort of."

"Listen, Harry, it's the Philippines, and they take their relationships seriously. Her ex-fiancé … it's all about his pride and trying to express his anger."

"Is that what it is?" Harry asked curiously.

"In their culture, it's all about how they look in front of others. It would have been difficult for Clarisse too, she is probably embarrassed."

"Yeah, I think she is. So, what do I do?"

"Nothing, mate, just let it be and focus on your last day together," Matt said.

"OK, mate, that's good advice from a great friend."

"You know me, Harry, I'm always here to talk to you—anytime."

"By the way, I'm staying an extra two days."

"You told your boss?" Matt asked.

"Yes, but I am not sure what awaits me."

"Don't worry, mate—you won't lose your job. They need people like you."

"You think so?"

"Where are they going to find someone with your skills and knowledge? They'd just be annoyed, if anything. Don't worry about it. I can call your boss and speak to him … smooth things over?"

"Nah, it's fine, and thanks for helping out. I will see you when I get back."

"Goodnight, Harry, and take care—call me anytime, all right?"

"I know I can. Have a good night."

Harry could always trust Matt to give him a positive spin on life's events. He relied on his advice; Matt was a well-travelled man and understood many cultures. He had been to Manila to meet Alicia and was still in contact with her.

He understood the complexities of their culture and how it worked. He was more in tune with people and had greater social awareness. It's what you would expect from a person in a sales profession who has travelled throughout South-East Asia.

9 THE PELLEGRINA

Harry and Clarisse decided to have dinner at the hotel restaurant next to the main lobby. If he had not cancelled his flight back home, the special dinner would never have taken place. Harry had taken a big gamble with his job and did not know what awaited him upon his return. He had been with the company for a long time—he was regularly sought after by their competitors. His company was aware that people like Harry were not easy to find. He took a punt they would forgive him, and he'd get away with a slap on the wrist.

But in the back of his mind, there was a rebellious contempt—he did not care about the consequences. It was only a job, and if need be, he would find another one. It was not something he would have contemplated a month ago, far from it—the diligent, structured and routine person he was would not have allowed for it. He had changed his outlook on life, and it had taken a turn for the better. The material things underpinned by his career did not mean as much to him anymore. Harry could always find another job, a source of income or another way to live. Finding someone like Clarisse again was not a guarantee in life.

Clarisse had arrived at the restaurant to greet Harry at the entrance near the hotel foyer. Their table was located in the open area leading into the courtyard. It was a picturesque and romantic setting that was popular amongst lovers. It was a tropical courtyard—Harry noticed the sampaguita growing in the background. The fragrance of jasmine reminded him of Clarisse and their time together at her hometown.

All the tables were reserved by hotel guests dressed immaculately for their night out. Most couples chose this venue to share a special moment with their loved one. It could be a marriage proposal, engagement or wedding anniversary. Everyone had their love story to tell—every romance was different from the other. There were also foreign men with their partners, like Harry and Clarisse, celebrating their time together.

Clarisse looked immaculate, and he could not take his

eyes off her. She wore a short crimson dress with outlines of tropical leaves and palm trees. She was by far the best-looking girl in the restaurant and Harry was proud to be in her presence. Some men secretly glanced over their shoulder to peek at her when their partner was not looking—it was subtle but noticeable enough for Harry.

They settled in with a Chandon champagne; they lifted their glasses and toasted to their good fortune. Le Petit Chandon is a bottle of elegant Australian champagne with a balance of sweetness and aged complexity—perfect for their occasion. It also made Harry feel proud that this well-known local winery was exporting their product overseas.

"I was not supposed to be here tonight—according to my watch I should have been going through customs at the airport," Harry said.

"I thought I was going to be saying goodbye. But I am so happy to be here instead."

"I managed to get another two days. Not sure what will happen when I arrive home." He took another sip of his champagne. "Hmm, this is nice." He looked at Clarisse with glee and said, "And to be honest, it's the first time in my life that I don't care—they can do whatever they want with me."

"I prayed for you. Everything will be OK when you

return home," Clarisse said.

"Thank you so much for your thoughts." They smiled at each other and said nothing for a minute as they soaked up the atmosphere. They enjoyed each other's company and every moment was an occasion they cherished. As much as there was uncertainty around Harry's job, he believed meeting the right girl only happened once in a lifetime.

Some people spend their whole life looking for the right person and fail in their quest. There are people who let the perfect person go by thinking another one will take their place. How naïve that would seem when the ideal person never showed up. It was the mystery of life—a hard lesson that people learned. Harry was very cognisant of this.

"There is something I want to share with you ... a family secret that goes back to my great-grandmother," said Clarisse.

"OK ... tell me." He took another sip of champagne and waited.

She pulled out a fancy garment from her bag that was folded carefully in a white cotton mesh pouch containing a red cross sown onto it. It was handmade by a skilled artisan, and of the highest quality.

"This is called a pellegrina." She lifted it to chest

height to show its craftsmanship and elegance. The couples at the nearby tables looked around and glanced at it, recognising its significance. It was not something the ordinary person would possess. In a Catholic country where people took their religion seriously, this was a big deal. One girl from the table directly in front performed the sign of the cross while her partner followed suit.

"Where did you get the pellegrina?" Harry asked. He was intrigued by the reaction it conjured around them.

"This is the shoulder cape worn by a Catholic cardinal. Notice it's buttonless and in the traditional scarlet colour?"

"Oh yes, I remember that when I was at a Catholic school. But why show me this?"

Clarisse shifted in her seat to make herself more comfortable. "It belonged to my great-grandmother Elena, and just like the scarlet chair, it has been in our family for generations."

"Elena keeps popping up in mysterious ways," Harry said. She was a puzzling and surreptitious person with lots of folklore. Clarisse asked Harry if he wanted to hold the pellegrina.

"It feels very smooth and silky ... oh and look at the intricate stitching. It's divine," he said.

"The story of how she got the pellegrina is full of

mystique."

"I am curious."

"Yes, it happened when a bad energy entered her house and took over the scarlet chair."

"You're kidding me? Bad energy embodied by the chair?"

"The cardinal had to leave abruptly for an overseas posting to the Vatican, and before departing, he gave her the pellegrina as a blessing." Clarisse sipped on her champagne while a tear formed in her right eye.

"That's an amazing story."

"Yes—she kept it secret until her dying moments."

"It's possible the church found out about the pellegrina and that it had gone missing?" Harry asked curiously.

"That's what people were saying at the time." Clarisse fidgeted with the table napkin in front of her.

"Do you believe the story, or did someone make this up?"

"My mother has evidence—a black-and-white photo of Elena and the cardinal together. She also has the church records showing his posting to the Vatican."

"That's very compelling information."

"I don't want there to be any secrets between us, Harry. That's why I am telling this."

They were interrupted by the waiter asking for their food order—they decided to pause the conversation by nodding to each other discreetly.

"So, who is keeping this pellegrina?"

"My uncle Pablo is the caretaker—he keeps it locked away at home." Clarisse was starting to show early signs of being tipsy from the champagne. Harry thought she was cute. When she consumed alcohol, her already talkative self became more animated—she could be very entertaining.

"I don't mean to be a sticky beak, but shouldn't your mother keep it?"

"When I was growing up, my mother had it removed from the drawer in the backroom with the scarlet chair."

"Was there a reason for that?"

"She told me strange things were happening in the room. Once she found the pellegrina pinned to the wall as though it was stuck."

"That is scary."

"It's superstition, Harry—it depends on how much you want to believe."

Harry poured more champagne into his glass as he felt he needed another dose. "I'm not into superstitions, but I respect your culture and what it means."

"My mother felt the pellegrina was blessed and that it

was fighting with the negative energy from the chair."

"A spiritual war between good and bad?"

"Something like that." She folded the pellegrina very neatly and carefully back into the pouch. She kissed it and performed the sign of the cross. The other couples seated across from them did precisely the same. It was an uncanny feeling, and it gave Harry the shivers.

"Your uncle Pablo doesn't mind you taking it?"

"He gave it to me before leaving at the bus terminal—he said it would help both of us."

"That's nice of him to think about us that way. I like your uncle Pablo, he is a good man, he's always looking out for you."

The waiter delivered their food, and the smell was so inviting they could barely wait to start eating. Harry had ordered a local dish that was oxtail with a creamy peanut sauce. Clarisse had settled on a rice dish with vegetables and pork ribs.

"Putting all the superstitions aside—I love the food in your country," Harry said while gesturing with his fork.

"I know how to make that dish you're eating."

"If you can make it like this then I am a lucky man," Harry said enthusiastically.

The champagne was starting to take effect on Harry, and his personality took on a more humorous character.

They told funny stories about their families and laughed throughout the night. Somehow, his experience with Clarisse had shown another side of him. In the short time they had known one another she had changed him forever. Harry was unleashing his inhibitions, prepared to see the world differently. He was ready to take a punt or a risk on something worthwhile.

Before the night was over, Clarisse invited Harry for a day out to see the historic centre of the City of Affection. They would visit the former Spanish fort and Manila Cathedral where Clarisse planned to have the pellegrina blessed. Harry was looking forward to the day out. It would be his second-last day in Manila and visiting a historical tourist site full of history and culture suited him. Harry would go anywhere with her—it didn't matter what she suggested, he would go along for the ride.

Harry escorted Clarisse to the front entrance of the hotel. They kissed each other on the cheek, hugged and said goodbye. Clarisse stepped into the cab and pulled down the window, blowing a kiss with her hand more than once with an electric smile. He reciprocated with a flying kiss as he pointed his hands towards her.

The people around them watched with glee and smiled, caught up in the emotion between two lovers. It's not something Harry would generally do, but the

Chandon was having an effect, and he was uncharacteristically letting loose. He had found a side to him he wanted to explore and unleash to the world. It was the real Harry coming out and not the one bound by controlled rituals and routine. He was done with the old Harry.

10 WITHIN THE WALLS

Harry was looking forward to his day in Manila. For the first time since his arrival, he was going to be a tourist for the day. He enjoyed reading about the history of South-East Asia and wanted to see the Spanish influence in Manila. He had prepared an itinerary that would take them to several historical sites. He was surprised to find out that Clarisse had never visited these places of importance, considering she was a local. It was almost like saying that Harry never visited the Sydney Harbour Bridge. He found it odd, but it was not unusual for locals not to explore their heritage.

The first stop was Manila Cathedral, where Clarisse was going to have the pellegrina blessed for her uncle Pablo. After that, it was the old Spanish fort at the fortified city of Intramuros (within the walls). That would include a walk around the Spanish streets and a ride on a traditional horse and cart. The last stop was Manila Bay, where Clarisse insisted on watching the best sunset in the world. She said a lot of couples frequent Manila Bay to view the sunset. Harry felt it sounded romantic and suggested they have dinner at one of the many restaurants along the bay afterwards.

Clarisse was on time with the cab, and he was not kept waiting—a stark difference to the second time they met. She wound down her window and waved at him to step inside. She showed no signs of being in a small incident the day before. The bandage next to her eye was gone, and there was no sign of swelling.

She was wearing a smooth lilac jersey dress without any prints. It was a tight fit just above her knees, and it emphasised her slender and perfect bodyline. Rather than wavy curls, she opted to tie her hair back in a flat and dead-straight style with an embroidered ribbon. She resembled a beautiful Spanish flamenco dancer—he could not stop gazing at her until Clarisse snapped him out of it and told him to hurry.

"Good morning, Harry," Clarisse said. She kissed him on the cheek and moved close to him while readjusting the seat belt.

"You look terrific today, and I like your hair."

"Thank you, Harry. It took me a while to prepare my hair this morning … it has to be styled in a particular way—are we going to Manila Cathedral first?"

"Yes, that is the first stop on our itinerary."

"You are so organised," Clarisse said. She tended to go with the flow without the need of a list to keep her in check.

"Yep, after that, Intramuros … if that's OK?"

"That's fine by me—and considering I have lived in this city for many years, I have never been to any of these places before."

"I think it will be interesting to learn about the rich history of your country," Harry affirmed.

"I think you know more about our history than I do." They both smiled, realising how ironic it was. Clarisse leaned closer to Harry and held on to his arm. Harry couldn't help noticing the jasmine scent that filled the back seat with its addictive fragrance. It was a pleasant reminder of her mother's garden back in her hometown.

The cab left the hotel for the main thoroughfare and onto the street towards the cathedral.

"So, what do you know about Manila Cathedral?" Clarisse asked.

"Is this a test?"

"No, just wondering if you studied up on it?"

"Well, I did actually—it is known as the Cathedral of the Immaculate Conception, after the Blessed Virgin Mary; it is in the walled city of Intramuros. Initially built in 1571 and rebuilt after an earthquake damaged it."

"That's very good, you like your history." Clarisse was surprised by his knowledge of history.

"I can tell you more if you like?"

"That's more than enough," Clarisse said, impressed by his retention of information.

Harry was looking forward to visiting this church of cultural significance. They were dropped off near the main entrance of the cathedral and made their way steadily to the large doors covered in stained-glass depictions of the Virgin Mary. It was a magnificent church with a marble floor and columns that led to the high altar. The central nave had high, vaulted ceilings that created an atmosphere of heaven and spiritual being.

"This church is so impressive," Harry said. He looked around with a 360-degree turn before focusing on the iron gates near the high altar. "It has a feeling I have not encountered before, like being at peace with oneself."

Clarisse removed the pouch from her bag containing the pellegrina and unfolded it. "Should we take it to the steps of the altar and have it blessed?"

"Yes, I think that's the holiest place in the church." Harry glanced over towards Clarisse and asked her to take the lead. "Have you thought of a prayer?"

"My uncle Pablo gave me some words to say in our native language—you may not understand what I am saying."

He took Clarisse's hand, and they walked together to the iron gates near the altar. As they came nearer to the steps, an elderly priest approached them politely and in an unassuming way. He adjusted his glasses and leaned forward to inspect the pellegrina.

"I have not seen one of these for a long time. They don't make them like this anymore." He raised his hand with an open palm and leaned forward. "Can I hold it?"

"Yes, Father, of course," Clarisse said.

"My goodness, this is the old-style pellegrina, and it would have belonged to a cardinal." He turned the pellegrina over and inspected the garment around the collar. "Here it is, the letters 'AJR'; that would have been the initials of the cardinal."

Harry and Clarisse looked at each other, unsure of what to say next. "I have never seen those initials before," she said.

"It was done that way on purpose—somewhat of an identifier in case it got lost or mixed up."

"You know a lot about the pellegrina?" Clarisse asked.

"The last time I witnessed one like this was when I was a young altar boy, and ever since I have become intrigued by the symbolism and beauty of the clothing—call it a hobby." The priest folded it back together and handed it to Clarisse. "Can I ask where you got it from? It's unusual to have this type of garment outside the church."

"Well ..."

"I promise I won't tell anyone," the priest interrupted.

"It belonged to my great-grandmother, and it was a gift."

"I see—she must have been an extraordinary woman for a cardinal to gift her this piece." The priest had a smirk on his face, and he nodded his head. "It's OK; we are aware within the Catholic church that some cardinals had friendships during their tenure. Nothing untoward or scandalous, by the way."

She tried to change the topic and said, "We have come here to have it blessed today."

"I don't think I am worthy of that; only another cardinal or the Pope can bless it."

"Who blessed this pellegrina originally?"

"Oh yes, all pellegrinas are blessed by the pontiff before they are issued—this one would have been no different."

"Oh, my goodness. I had no idea." Clarisse sighed in awe of what she had learned.

"But there is nothing wrong with saying a prayer to reconnect with God," said the priest.

"Can we do that with you?" Clarisse asked.

"Of course you can. Why don't we kneel here and all three of us hold the pellegrina while I make a special prayer?"

They all kneeled on the steps of the altar while the priest raised the pellegrina above his shoulders, towards the cross of Jesus Christ overlooking the altar. It was a special prayer delivered in Latin. Although Harry and Clarisse did not understand the prayer, they liked it and felt it befitting of the pellegrina.

"My dear, you have a note in your hand with a prayer written down—do you want to say those devoted words?" the priest said.

"Yes, my uncle Pablo will be happy with that," Clarisse said. She took the paper note with the prayer and read it in her language.

"Those are gracious words, my dear, and only a cardinal could have written them," the priest said.

Clarisse and Harry looked at one another in dismay. Had the elderly priest stumbled onto something they had missed altogether?

"Was Elena's prayer originally written by the cardinal?" Clarisse whispered to Harry.

The elderly priest had to leave and excused himself, thanking both of them for the pleasure of touching the original pellegrina.

"Oh, and by the way—did I mention I am a religious historian for the church?"

"No," Clarisse responded.

"The initials AJR stand for Antonio Junior Rodriguez—cardinal of South Manila. He became one of our most respected cardinals in the Vatican." He bowed to the pellegrina and nodded to both of them before making his way to the back of the church.

They both took a seat at the front pew and reflected on what had just happened. They had come to Manila Cathedral to bless the pellegrina, and through fate, they met an elderly priest who recognised the symbolic cloth. And not only did he appreciate its significance—but he was also able to trace the initials back to the owner: a famous and well-respected cardinal noted in historical records.

Mystified by the experience and chance encounter with the priest, Clarisse kneeled before the altar and performed the sign of the cross. A tear gently rolled down her face as they walked to the entrance. They did not say anything—comfortable with the information they had received from the elderly priest. It vindicated the story of Elena and how the pellegrina fell into the family's hands. They walked past the main entrance holding hands while Harry comforted her in the best way he could; understanding that superstition can have its foundations in real events unbeknown to anyone.

They left the church for the Spanish fort of Intramuros. The cathedral was walking distance to the fort, so they set off on foot.

"Oh, look there, a Spanish horse cart. Want to go for a ride?" Harry said.

The driver waved in their direction to encourage them. "Sure, Harry, I have not been on a *kalesa* since I was a child." She took hold of his arm, tugging it so they could catch a ride.

"What is a kalesa?" Harry asked.

"It's what we call a single horse-drawn cart, and it comes from our Spanish heritage."

"It's perfect for the walled city because it's laid out in the old Spanish way."

The streets were paved with old black stone and the houses built with the same distinct Spanish architecture of the time.

They stepped inside the kalesa and took their seats

next to each other. It had two wheels and two rows of chairs that could accommodate four people. The driver was sitting on a block of wood located at the front of the cart near the horse. With the crack of his whip, the carriage started rolling at a steady pace through the Spanish street. The original stone road built was bumpy in parts, and it jolted them around the seat. Harry didn't mind because with every bump, Clarisse was closer to him to the point they were almost cuddling.

The driver asked where they were heading. Clarisse informed him to go towards the old Spanish fort two blocks away. In the meantime, the kalesa took a tourist route through the old Spanish quarter, and it was like being in another country. The ride in the horse-drawn cart had made Clarisse forget about their encounter in the cathedral. She was looking forward to the rest of her day with Harry at the walled city.

"Here we are." Harry gave the driver a tip, and they made their way to the old Spanish fort.

"You can see the entrance of the Pasig River," Clarisse said.

The fort was damaged during the Second World War, and parts of it had been restored to its original architecture. However, for Harry, it was a journey through history that triggered his senses. He liked being part of the past—preferring to see it first-hand rather than reading about it in history books with flashy pictures.

"It's like being in the middle of a Spanish town, but we are in South-East Asia," Harry said.

"I have never been here before, and I can't believe how nice it is." Clarisse pointed to the Spanish guard wearing the uniform of a conquistador. He was handing out brochures to the tourists with an appealing smile. "Come to think about it, my friends have never been here; it would never have crossed their minds to visit."

"Something only the tourist does—right?"

"Yeah, something like that. But Harry, I want to thank you for taking me here. I feel immersed in my culture and heritage."

"It's no problem, I'm happy to be your tour guide for the day." They both laughed and kept walking towards the main entrance of the Spanish fort.

Harry picked up a brochure and waved to the guard at the main gate while other tourists took photos. He opened the first page of the brochure and read the introduction to Clarisse.

Fort Santiago is a citadel first built by Spanish navigator and governor Miguel López de Legazpi for the newly established city of Manila in the Philippines. The defence fortress is part of the structures of the walled city of Manila referred to as Intramuros.

The fort is one of the most important historical sites in Manila. Several lives were lost in its prisons during the Spanish Empire and World War II. José Rizal, one of the Philippine national heroes, was imprisoned here before his execution in 1896. The Rizal Shrine museum displays memorabilia of the hero in their collection and the fort features, embedded onto the ground in bronze, his footsteps representing his final walk from his cell to the location of the actual execution.

It is only a few metres away from the Manila Cathedral and the Palacio del Gobernador. (Wikipedia.org)

"I studied this at school, but I can't say I remember it that well. It feels different being here—the way you read that makes it even more interesting."

"Want to take a seat in that garden café, next to the souvenir shop?" Harry said. He was starting to get peckish and felt like an iced tea.

"Sure, I wouldn't mind a drink. It's sticky and humid today."

"I'm not used to this weather." He pinched his polo top to show the uncomfortable sweat that was starting to build on his back.

Clarisse laughed. "There is a fan in that café—it will cool you down."

"Well, guess what? I'm going to sit right in front of it."

They made their way to the small café and sat down next to the fan.

"Tomorrow is your last day," Clarisse said.

"Thanks for the reminder—I'm not looking forward to leaving. I may not have a job to go back to."

"I'm sure you're overplaying it. It's not the first time someone has overstayed a holiday."

"If they want to get rid of me, that's fine. I will catch the next flight back here, to the City of Affection." Harry was silent and paused for a while. The possibility of losing his job was a dilemma. But nothing made him feel more anxious than the thought of leaving Clarisse behind. His affection for her had grown considerably in the last week. There was nothing about her he disliked, except for the superstitions—that was something he was going to have to live with.

"I have something from my mother; she asked me to give it to you before you leave."

"Your mother ... really?" Harry shifted in his chair and crossed his legs. "I thought your mother didn't ..."

"Didn't like you?" Clarisse placed an ornate gold cross

in his hand. "It will remind you of my family."

"Clarisse, this gold cross is too much—your mother shouldn't have."

"I know she was hard on you. However, she realised you're a perfect gentleman and how you respect me." She put the cross in the palm of his hand and gently closed it. "She wanted you to have it. Here … keep it in a safe place."

Harry was stunned into silence and didn't know what to say. All he could do was admire the gold cross in his hand.

"I can't remember the last time someone gave me something special like this before. I know it came from the heart and I want you to thank your mother—tell her I will always wear it."

Clarisse burst into tears and put her head on his chest.

"I don't want you to leave, Harry. Stay a little longer?"

Harry paused and thought about what he was about to say. He put his arms around her. It was going to be difficult for Clarisse to let Harry go; even if it wasn't permanently, it still made her feel sick.

"I have already overstayed my holiday, Clarisse, and could lose my job. I need to go back home—I need you to be strong."

"I know … you have done a lot already—I should be

less selfish," Clarisse said.

"I will come back."

"Will you?"

"Yes, it's only an eight-hour flight away—it's a small world." Harry smiled and nodded.

They ordered tea and spent the next hour talking about all sorts of things. They enjoyed each other's company and the conversation flowed naturally. That is what made their relationship work and grow freely. They liked sitting around and discussing a variety of issues— even the history lessons from Harry were entertaining and animated in the way he presented them.

After they finished the tour of the old Spanish fort, they decided to rest before meeting for dinner in Manila Bay. Clarisse wanted Harry to see the sunset over the bay that had become a popular place for lovers.

During the tour of the fort, Clarisse asked Harry to stand by one of the old original cannons overlooking the entrance to the Pasig river. It was a picturesque view overlooking the entrance to Manila Bay. Harry stepped onto the platform holding the barrel and posed with a two-finger salute. Clarisse thought it was funny—the cheeky side of him was coming out.

They moved on to the gallows where an iron-gated entrance provided a backdrop for an eerie feeling. This was the place where prisoners were incarcerated in atrocious conditions awaiting execution by firing squad. Harry walked up to the gate and grasped hold of it, looking into the blackness of the underground prison. He could imagine the screams of hundreds of people that had passed through this guardhouse incarcerated and about to die. Harry asked Clarisse to take a photo of him standing next to the iron gate, but she refused—concerned about upsetting the spirits of the dead. It was another superstition he had to accept and let be.

"I think it's time we left," said Clarisse.

"Yes, we should prepare for Manila Bay."

Harry hailed down a kalesa at the front entrance of the fort. They would return to the cathedral where cabs were parked waiting for passengers. It was the same kalesa that brought them to the fort—the driver recognised them and smiled. Clarisse provided Harry with instructions on how to get to Manila Bay from his hotel by offering a Google-Maps link on his phone of the exact drop-off. It was a twenty-minute drive by cab. They would meet at five in the afternoon in front of the main entrance to the Mall of Asia—directly in front of Manila Bay Walk.

Harry managed to find his way to the Mall of Asia after deciding to use a trusted hotel driver instead of catching a cab. He stood at the entrance to the great mall and waited for Clarisse to arrive. It was a busy shopping complex with swarms of people going in and out. It was popular with foreigners, who made him feel more comfortable—that is, he was not the only one who looked different.

Clarisse arrived by cab and was ten minutes late. Harry understood what the traffic was like in Manila and did not mind waiting. They decided to walk briskly from the Mall of Asia to Manila Bay as the sun was starting to set. They probably had twenty minutes left before it got dark. Clarisse was confident they would make it in time to see the final stage of the sunset. They walked from the mall to the overpass leading directly to the bay. Harry could see the picturesque bay walk in front of him.

It was a typical warm night with a very slight sea breeze, and not a cloud in sight. The sunset was a blend of perfect red and orange rays reflecting across the bay. The colour became more intense as the sun descended further over the horizon. Harry could not get over the size of the sun; it resembled a brilliant orange hanging from a tree. Couples lined up the main pathway everywhere— some standing and holding hands while others sat under trees holding each other.

Not far from where they stood was a small barrier no more than half a metre high. It was an old stone wall that protected people from the rocky entrance to the bay. Harry jumped on the wall with one big leap and positioned himself to get a better view.

"It looks better up here," Harry said, lifting both his arms in the air. "Here, give me your hand."

Clarisse thought about it at first and then succumbed to his charm. "OK … don't let go."

He lifted her onto the stone wall, careful not to lose their footing.

"It does look better up here—don't let go," she said.

Other couples that looked on thought it was a good idea and followed suit. Jumping onto the stone wall was more adventurous, and it caught on quickly. All of a sudden, more than ten couples stood on the wall and raised their arms while taking selfies with their phone.

Harry held Clarisse around the shoulder while she placed her head on his chest. Nature's beauty was doing most of the talking—the sun was drowning into the endless sea as the warm rays of orange and red protruded through the small line of clouds like a scene from heaven. Harry had never seen a sunset like this before; he did not live near the equator, and the tilt of the Earth provided a unique intensity that made Manila Bay special at this time of day.

11 THE CLEANSING

Clarisse received a call from her mother early in the morning that Marjorie had taken ill and was in hospital. Marlita did not explain what the illness was or how Marjorie got sick. The only information she provided was that Marjorie collapsed in the backroom next to the scarlet chair.

She did not need any further clarification and could read between the lines. Marjorie had attempted to access the energy of the scarlet chair. For some unknown reason, Marjorie had had a strong feeling that something was about to happen and sought a premonition from the scarlet chair. Clarisse felt confused—Marjorie had not met her chatmate personally; they were only talking to each other on Skype. Was there something else in her life she was not aware of? Was Marjorie keeping a secret? Why would she go to such lengths to use the negative energy of the chair after what Clarisse had already suffered? Marjorie was always out there, pushing the boundaries and taking unnecessary risks. Even though she witnessed the effects of the scarlet chair on Clarisse first-hand, it would not have prevented her from trying it out herself. Maybe she was naïve and just wanted to see if the superstition about the chair was real. With her light-hearted approach to life, one could never know what Marjorie was thinking.

Clarisse was undecided whether to take the first available bus back home to see Marjorie. However, she faced another problem—Harry was leaving at 9:30 p.m. that evening and had to be at the airport by 6 p.m. Getting back to Manila would require a quick turnaround. It depended on the bus not encountering unusual traffic delays—something that could not be guaranteed any time of the year. For Clarisse to have enough time to get to the airport with Harry meant everything had to run smoothly. That said, she would have a three-hour turnaround to see her mother and Marjorie before returning.

Clarisse picked up her mobile phone and looked up Harry's number.

"Maybe I should say nothing to Harry about the sudden need to go home?" she said with her fingers on the dial pad. "I don't want to cause him any worry on his last day." They had arranged to meet in front of the hotel at 5:30 p.m. and travel to the airport together. If everything went according to plan, she would meet her deadline, and there would be no need for explanations. She knew how sceptical Harry was about the superstition.

"Damn … I can't lie to him." Clarisse immediately dialled Harry's number.

"Harry, it's me, Clarisse. I need to say something important." Her voice cracked as she prepared to tell him the news.

"Sure, Clarisse, what is it?" Harry could sense her discomfort from the tone in her voice.

"I just got word from my mother that Marjorie is in hospital. I don't know what to do."

"What do you mean, Clarisse? She is a close friend and has done so much for you."

"If I go to see her today, I may not make it back to Manila on time to take you to the airport … everything would have to go exactly according to plan."

"I know what the traffic is like here and it's unpredictable," Harry said.

Clarisse sat on the side of her bed and clasped her

forehead. "I don't know what to do."

Harry paused for a moment to gather his thoughts and said, "Clarisse, don't worry about me. You're acting if it's the last time you will see me. I suggest you go and see Marjorie in hospital. If you leave now, it will allow enough time to get back."

"Are you sure?"

"Of course I'm sure. You have known her longer than me—I know how much she means to you."

"Thank you so much, Harry," Clarisse sighed.

"Call me and let me know how everything is … Promise?"

"I promise …"

Clarisse quickly got her belongings together and jumped into the first available cab for the bus terminal. The next bus was leaving in thirty minutes and time was of the essence.

On the bus to her mother's house, Clarisse had the jitters, butterflies in her stomach and felt restless. She wanted to be strong but was finding it difficult to cope. The man of her dreams was leaving tonight, and her much-loved friend was in the hospital recovering from a mystery illness. It could not have happened at a worse time, and she felt unlucky in love. There was always something waiting to happen, and every time she met someone special, another situation threatened to ruin it altogether. Perhaps that was the real superstition—a love-seeking curse to all the family members for generations to come.

The bus trip went without a hiccup and upon arrival at the bus station, her uncle Pablo was waiting with the sidecar, ready to whisk her away to the hospital. He did not say too much about Marjorie and focused on getting her to the hospital quickly. Her uncle Pablo was a skilled driver and knew all the shortcuts to beat the traffic. He could cut off fifteen minutes on the average journey. Pushing his way through traffic with quick turns and a burst of acceleration, he would turn into alleyways and narrow streets to avoid the bottlenecks.

Clarisse was used to the rollercoaster ride and would always hold on tightly to the metal frame of the sidecar to keep it steady. She would lean towards the side that her uncle Pablo was turning to help him with the momentum required as they worked in tandem to optimise the sidecar's performance. It was a technique she learned at a young age, and although it had a practical use, she also enjoyed the challenge it provided.

Upon arriving at the hospital, they walked briskly to the shared ward where Marjorie was resting. Her uncle Pablo struggled to keep up with her but waved her on. He did not want to slow Clarisse down due to his ageing legs and slower step.

Clarisse swept past the nurses' station directly for room 205, creating a draught strong enough to make the paperwork flutter off the main counter. The nurses that were lazing about turned their heads intuitively and moaned in annoyance. She flung open the door to see her mother and aunty sitting by Marjorie's bedside, holding rosary beads and praying. She was sedated and could barely open her eyes. Clarisse sensed that Marjorie could feel her presence and caressed her forehead.

She leaned over the bed and held on to her hard, teary-eyed. Clarisse was concerned for Marjorie and did not want her to go through the same recovery that she had to endure for two weeks.

"What have you done?" Clarisse said.

Marjorie moaned, acknowledging Clarisse's presence, but made no sense as she continued to hold her hand.

"You know that chair is bad and you saw it with your own eyes. Why did you go there?" Clarisse sobbed in anger but also with heartfelt emotion. She blamed herself for bringing Marjorie into the superstition of the secret chair. Spellbound by the negative energy of the scarlet chair; she knew what Marjorie was going through. Clarisse was so caught up in spending time with Harry that she had forgotten about the impact it had on herself. Marjorie's incident was bringing back painful memories.

"Mother, did you have any inclination this was happening?"

"My dear, we had no idea she would do this after what she experienced with you."

Clarisse sat on the side of the bed next to Marjorie and placed her hands on her forehead. "I don't believe it had to do with a man," she said. "If anything, it was the superstition itself she was testing—to see how far she could take it."

"She doesn't have anyone special in her life," Marlita said.

"I know she is the curious type, Mother, and always out there trying something new, but this is taking it too far."

"I don't want to argue, my dear, but is it any different than when *you* sat on the chair?" Marlita said provocatively.

There was a deafening silence in the room, and they looked at each other. Marjorie's actions, as unthinkable as they may appear to the neutral observer, were no different to Clarisse's—even if they'd had different motives.

Marjorie was sedated and struggled to keep her eyes open, slipping in and out of consciousness intermittingly.

However, she was aware Clarisse was next to her as she grasped her hand silently, not wanting to let go.

"Isn't Harry leaving tonight?" Marlita asked.

"Yes, Mother … I don't know if I will make it on time for his departure. I need to be at the hotel around 5:30 p.m."

"He doesn't know about Marjorie?"

"Yes, I told him I was coming here to see Marjorie." She stood up from her chair, looking for a glass of water. "Every time I mention that damn chair, he becomes more curious and he's not into superstition."

"I understand, my dear; it's not an easy thing to explain—better left alone and kept in the family."

"Well, Mother, this is what happens when people outside our immediate family learn about the chair. It's my fault, I brought Marjorie into it … now look at her."

"You're too hard on yourself, Clarisse—you can't control everyone." Marlita looked directly at her. "I tried so hard to separate that chair from your lives and the people around us."

"I know, Mother, I'm just emotional at the moment."

"Listen, dear … we can take care of Marjorie for now. Go back to Manila and catch the next bus. If all goes to plan, you will arrive with time to spare."

"I can't leave Marjorie like this."

"Clarisse, if Marjorie found out you did not get back to see Harry, she would get mad."

Clarisse paused for a while, looked at Marjorie and caressed her forehead again. "That's true, Mother, she would get upset and say I was not thinking straight."

She took her mother's advice and wished Marjorie a speedy recover. Her uncle Pablo escorted her downstairs to the sidecar for the ten-minute drive home. Clarisse had unfinished business with the chair and wanted to attend to it immediately before catching the next bus to Manila.

Upon arriving at her home, there was an eerie silence she had not experienced before. Did the scarlet chair sense she was coming?

"Uncle Pablo, wait for me here for fifteen minutes. It won't take long," she said.

Clarisse was on a mission—there were going to be fireworks, whether the chair liked it or not. She bolted through the back door, heading straight for the backroom with the scarlet chair. She dropped her backpack and unzipped the front compartment. She tugged it open and delicately removed the white woven pouch with the gold cross engraved at the front. She opened the pouch carefully by loosening the genuine pearl string—and there it was, the pellegrina in all its glory. Clarisse carefully removed the pellegrina and placed it around her shoulders just like a cardinal of the Catholic church. She took a few deep breaths to calm her racing heart.

She heard a screech coming from the room, and it was the same sound that Harry questioned her about many times. She attempted to open the door, but something was holding it back. It was not locked, which made it more surreal. She gave it a big shove and managed to move it ajar. The chair was fighting back, and it was not happy. The chair's energy transcended from another dimension and was starting to reveal itself.

The superstition had a secret that not even her mother was cognisant of. Clarisse had worked out that it was no accident the pellegrina was given to Elena by the cardinal—it was to ward off the negative energy in their home. If a negative force confronted it, the pellegrina would fight back and cleanse it. Was the scarlet chair already evil and possessing negative energy when Elena was alive? Evil spirits and bad energies don't have a time frame on Earth like us mortal souls. They can drag on for centuries, applying their misery from one generation to another until the final confrontation.

Clarisse stood in front of the chair, eyes gazing, staunch and determined. The pellegrina was shaking with an intense vibration she had not experienced before. It flapped around her head, continually covering her eyes deliberately to block her view. She was holding the pellegrina down with both hands to maintain eye contact with the chair. The fragrance of the jasmine sambac had turned into the stench again. Each picture frame containing photos of dead relatives dropped face down on the console table—clatter, clatter, clatter. Clarisse was steadfast in her resolution and carried on.

A loud screech gave way to a gust of putrid cold air that blasted against the side of her face and her arms, sending a shivering chill through her body. The scarlet chair trembled as the legs bounced on the wooden floor like a Spanish flamenco dancer. It had shifted ninety degrees and was now facing away from her, towards the fallen picture frames. Was the chair seeking help from one of the dead relatives and was it trying to communicate? Clarisse trembled but maintained her fury on the chair.

The confrontation continued for another minute until a deafening loud bang echoed across the room—and then silence, serenity and fragrance filled the room all over again. Was it a trick? Was the chair trying to trick her? Clarisse waited for ten minutes to see if the chair was cunningly trying to outmanoeuvre her. There was still nothing, and the room remained serene in her presence. Clarisse stepped to the chair and kissed it, making the sign of the holy cross. Had she beaten the negative force with the power of the pellegrina? She reached for the cross at the altar and removed it, placing it on the chair, and kneeled.

The door slammed shut behind her with a reverberating bang that filled the room with an echo—a voracious sound like a growling dog filtered out from the room. Clarisse could not see where the sound was coming from—it was everywhere. The air was becoming thin and cold as a slight mist emitted from beneath the chair. She felt like choking—but realised it was a trick, designed to make her panic. The air was breathable despite the haze that was starting to form.

A picture frame dislodged from the wall and flung across the room, narrowly missing her shoulder. It smashed into the brick wall behind her, shattering into pieces on the floor. The console table rattled with a fit of anger, dropping all the remaining picture frames on the floor beneath it. The chair was angry and desperate—not happy that Clarisse had forced its hand. The putrid stench of rotting flowers returned to the room exacerbated by the cold mist.

"Help Me, Uncle!" Clarisse yelled from inside the room.

Uncle Pablo could hear the commotion from outside

and rushed to the door of the room where Clarisse was battling the evil energy. He tried to force it open, but something was holding it back. He pushed and shoved with his shoulder—each time applying greater force to dislodge it. He could not cope with the physical strength required due to his ageing body.

Uncle Pablo had no strength left in him to force open the door and sought help by getting a crowbar from the garden shed. He was going to force the door open and dislodge it from the hinges. He jammed the crowbar into a narrow gap in the door and heaved until the door succumbed. He flung the door open and dashed towards Clarisse—avoiding another picture frame by the skin of his teeth. She was lying on the floor with the pouch in her hand—almost immobilised as though frozen it time; the chair had taken a grip on her.

"Remove the pellegrina," Uncle Pablo shouted.

Clarisse managed to remove the pellegrina from around her shoulders. The sight of the holy garment angered the chair—it started to rotate anticlockwise at various intervals.

"Throw the pellegrina on the chair and hold it down," Uncle Pablo instructed with an authoritative voice.

"I can't, Uncle—it's holding me back."

"It has to come from you, or it won't confront it …

keep trying," he said.

Clarisse focused intensely by closing her eyes to build the energy she needed and launched herself onto the chair face down. With the pellegrina firmly in her hands, she forced it into the chair and held it down with both hands. The chair reacted by rattling intensely, rocking side to side to dislodge the pellegrina. A wrinkled hand of an older woman rose from the chair in a circular motion and tugged on her dress—ripping it to one side.

"It's tearing my dress!" Clarisse yelled. "Get this hand off me!"

A yellow-tinged glow formed around the outside of the pellegrina like a shamanic aura.

"Keep holding it down to absorb the spirit," said Uncle Pablo.

Clarisse was brave and intent on defeating the chair as she held down the pellegrina with an inner strength well beyond her normal abilities. The chair rallied and tried hopelessly to maintain its power as it slowly descended into nothing.

With her hair messed up and dress torn to one side, Clarisse stood upright and hugged Uncle Pablo. He was always there for her, no matter the circumstances.

"We have beaten it, Uncle," she whispered.

"Yes, my dear ... it's gone. I can tell this time."

The room had turned serene again, and the stench of mist had gone. However, the remnants of the shattered picture frames and the indentations in the wooden floor from the rattling legs of the chair remained—a reminder of the battle that had taken place.

After ten minutes, she glanced at her phone to check the time. Clarisse had to get to the bus terminal. It was going to be touch and go, but she had done this trip countless times. Barring any significant road accident, she estimated to arrive with time to spare. Fortunately for her, it was the quiet time of year and a weekday. She anticipated normal traffic conditions for Manila. She folded the pellegrina back into the pouch and pelted through the back door to her uncle Pablo, who was already waiting and seated on his motorbike, ready to go.

"Here, Uncle Pablo, take the pellegrina." Clarisse took a couple of deep breaths. "I had it blessed at Manila Cathedral."

Her uncle Pablo smiled and thanked her for doing him a favour. The pellegrina belonged to him, and he would put it away for safekeeping again as he had always done. He was aware the next bus was leaving in twenty minutes, and Clarisse was on a tight schedule. He expertly drove her through shortcuts and alleyways to cut through the congested intersections. They arrived at the bus terminal with enough time to purchase her ticket and board the bus. They had made good time and arrived at the bus terminal with time to spare.

"Thank you so much, Uncle Pablo, and please say goodbye to everyone—give my love to Aunty." Clarisse kissed her uncle Pablo on the cheek and hugged him.

Uncle Pablo nodded, and, like always, he was sad to see her leave.

She then asked her uncle Pablo to turn his head towards her. She placed her hand on his face and leaned forward to whisper in his ear,

"I cleansed the chair, and I beat it today. The negative energy is gone ... gone forever."

Her uncle Pablo nodded and smiled back at her. He understood what it meant for the family that she had eliminated the negative force in the chair that had dogged it for generations. He waved to Clarisse and wished her good fortune as she boarded the bus. She was on her way to Manila and to see Harry.

Clarisse faced a dilemma that had turned into guilt. She had not mentioned anything specific about the scarlet chair and the family superstition to Harry, preferring to deflect his questions at every chance. She also knew that Harry was interested—backing away from any discussion because he could sense it was a sore point. But had Clarisse left it too late? What was the point confessing it to Harry on their way to the airport? Her other option was to hope he would return to Manila in a couple of months to visit, providing her enough time to explain everything in detail.

The bus was sixty minutes out from her town and heading for a notorious stretch of underdeveloped road that usually got clogged with traffic. Clarisse knew the route the bus took like the back of her hand, having completed this journey at least one hundred times since she was a child. She looked ahead as the bus got nearer to the notorious stretch and she could see some commotion—flashing lights of vehicles; however, they were not construction trucks. She gulped, thinking the worse, that perhaps an accident had occurred. The locals called this stretch of road 'Accident Alley' because of the risks drivers took to get ahead of the traffic. A combination of buses, trucks, cars, motorbikes and sidecars made it a driving hell that the local municipality had not yet managed to resolve. It was so bad they could not afford the expense to fix it all at once.

Traffic had come to a halt, and it was jammed—some people were out of their cars, smoking and waiting patiently for the traffic to clear. Clarisse's pulse was elevated, and the pounding beat of her heart echoed in her ears—she was starting to feel anxious. Had she made a blunder by deciding to go home? She began to question her judgement. At this rate, she would not make it in time to see Harry off. Clarisse could feel the sweat building on her forehead, and she started to shiver.

The bus was gridlocked for twenty minutes, and nothing was moving. Motorbike riders were taking risks by riding onto the pavement, to the detriment of pedestrians that waved and yelled at them. Mothers carrying children did not appreciate the motorbike riders putting them at risk.

What on earth do I do now? she thought. She was feeling helpless.

Clarisse dialled Harry's phone. She wanted to keep her promise and let him know how everything was going.

"Hi, Clarisse, how is everything?"

"I'm on my way back; there has been a slight delay one hour out of my town."

"Really? How bad is it?"

"All I can see are the lights of road vehicles ahead—I think there has been an accident. We have not moved for twenty minutes … not an inch."

"Oh, that does not sound too good." Harry paused for a moment, contemplating his thoughts. He could hear

Clarisse sobbing in the background. "How long can the delay last until it's too late to arrive in Manila?"

"Maybe another thirty minutes," she said with a croaking voice.

"It's OK, Clarisse. Stay calm. It may start moving again soon. Maybe they are clearing the broken-down car now, and it won't be long."

"OK, Harry, I will send a message once we get moving again." Although she was feeling better with the encouragement, there was also a source of apprehension.

The driver received a radio message from the control centre that a van had rolled over into a ditch on the side of the road. The emergency crews had finally lifted the van onto a tow truck. The traffic was expected to start moving anytime now, although at a slow pace initially. The bus driver communicated the news to the passengers, and there were smiles and sighs of relief all around. Clarisse checked the time, and even with the current delay, she would arrive in Manila with fifteen minutes to spare.

The rest of the bus trip back went smoothly, and the bus driver managed to make up lost time—scheduled to arrive at the bus terminal on time. Clarisse had been through so much that she was exhausted and fell asleep for the remainder of the journey.

Upon arriving at the bus terminal, she messaged Harry in advance that she was on her way to the hotel.

Clarisse checked her belongings in her backpack and ensured her gift for Harry was not damaged. It was a picture of them together, standing next to the Spanish guard at the entrance of Intramuros at the Spanish fort. She picked this photo because they both looked great— Harry was holding her tightly, they had big smiles, and it had a picturesque backdrop. She was hoping Harry would place her picture on his bedside table in an elegant white frame with the engraved words: 'The best love is the kind that awakens the soul.'

12 LOVE PLUS NOTHING

The hardest-learned lesson: that people only have their kind of love to give, not our kind.

Mignon McLaughlin

The cab arrived five minutes early, and Clarisse was happy to be on time. With all the things that could have gone wrong between travelling to her home and back again, it was remarkable how she made it on time to see Harry off at the airport. She firmly believed in her faith and that someone was watching over her today.

Harry was like clockwork, waiting at the front entrance of the hotel and ready to go. He was juggling his bags as he tried to coordinate all his belongings.

"Let me help with the luggage, sir," said the porter.

He managed to load everything into the boot of the cab and then waited, smiling at Harry.

Clarisse whispered to Harry, "You need to give him a small tip. Do you have twenty pesos?"

"Oh yes, I have it here," Harry said. He tipped the porter before stepping into the cab with Clarisse.

"I have a gift for you, Harry … it's something small to remember our time together," Clarisse said. She removed a parcel from her backpack; it was wrapped in silver paper and tied with a red ribbon.

"I can't open it now because I don't want to destroy the wrapping," Harry said.

"It's OK … open it up on the plane or when you get back. Don't forget to remove the picture of me on your bedside table and replace it with this one."

"So, it's a picture frame?"

"Not saying, it's a surprise," Clarisse said with a cheeky grin.

Harry took the parcel and placed it in his carry-on bag. "Thanks so much for the gift, I'm looking forward to opening it when I get back home." Harry smiled and looked at her in a presumptuous way. "So how did you know I had your picture on my bedside table?"

"Marjorie can't keep a secret," Clarisse said.

"Well, obviously my friend Matt told Alicia, and it got to you that way."

They both laughed realising how small the world was and how news could travel so far.

"I have a gift also," Harry said.

"A gift for me?" Clarisse was excited. "I didn't expect anything."

"I thought I would surprise you."

"I can't wait to see it."

"Well here it is, Clarisse, and here is a card."

"What's in the card? It's not my birthday."

"It's a going-away card to say thanks for everything."

Clarisse was silent and did not know what to say. The gesture from Harry had made her speechless.

"I guess I can't open it now?" The red box with a pink laced ribbon was the size of a jewellery case used for gold chains or pendants.

"Not now, but later … after I leave. Oh, and read my card at the same time."

"I don't know what to say." Clarisse could not handle the anticipation of opening the gift and shook it a few times next to her ear.

The experience of the last seven days came crashing down on her all at once. Harry would be leaving her in approximately one hour. At this point, she would have given anything for him to stay an extra couple of days—but she was aware he had already put himself at risk with his job by overstaying.

Clarisse casually put her head on his shoulder while holding on to her gift and card with both hands, her legs trembling slightly, but enough for Harry to notice.

At the intersection of a busy thoroughfare, a pretty little girl no more than ten years old was holding on to a chain of sampaguita flowers tied together. She raised them at Harry and knocked on the window several times, urging him to buy one. The cab driver advised him not to wind down the window because it was not safe. Harry was in a defiant mood, and unlike his conservative self, this time, he decided to throw caution to the wind. He pulled down the window and asked the little girl for the chain of sampaguita flowers. She put out her hand seeking money while cautiously lifting the sampaguita through the window.

"Here, Harry, give her these coins … it's twenty pesos," Clarisse said.

Harry placed the coins into the palms of the pretty little girl. She put the chain of flowers over Harry's head, smiled and nodded before disappearing into the traffic.

They could smell the jasmine scent of the petals as it

filled the cab with a lovely, relaxing fragrance.

"This is for you," Harry said, placing the flower chain over Clarisse's head like a classic Hawaiian lei.

"They smell so beautiful," she said.

"Nothing like your mother's flowers but I still like them."

"It was very spontaneous."

"Your culture has brought out the other side of me," Harry said.

"You're spoiling me so much today. Thanks for the flowers … they mean a lot to me."

Harry could see the street signs for Manila Airport and the planes taking off into the sunset in the distance. They were not far away now from the international airport departures drop-off. Clarisse was silent as she fiddled with the sampaguita around her neck. They did not talk at all for the last five minutes of the cab ride and held on to what precious moments they had remaining.

As the cab arrived at the bustling departures drop-off area, Harry's heart started racing, and he could feel it thumping against his chest. As he looked towards the entrance to the departure's hall, he knew his time with Clarisse was finally coming to an end. After the most amazing seven days of his life in Manila, he knew it was time to say goodbye to her.

"Sir, we have arrived. I will help you with your bags," said the taxi driver.

Harry was motionless—almost refusing to leave the cab and grabbing every moment with Clarisse. She was the bravest of the two—nudging Harry gently to get his luggage and then flinging the cab door open with her feet. The cab driver managed to access a trolley that was lying around nearby and assisted Harry load up his bags.

They pushed the trolley together through the main entrance to the departures hall carefully to ensure his luggage did not tip over onto the pavement. They both looked at each other intensely for a moment as they passed through the main door.

"So, looks like we are finally here," Clarisse said. She looked directly at Harry, teardrops cascading from her rosy cheeks. He had a feeling of disquiet and smiled at her.

"I am coming back," Harry said.

"That's what they all say, and then they never turn up."

"I mean it, Clarisse. Once I find out what's going on with my job, I will return."

"When?"

"Is three months too long?"

"No, it's not, because I will wait as long as it takes for

you to come back. Promise me?" She gave Harry a sincere, warm hug and put her head on his shoulder. "Promise me?"

Harry held her tight and whispered in her ear, "I promise."

There was a moment of silence, and all they could hear was the noise around them. They were unconcerned with anything else, and they focused on one another.

"I think I must go, Clarisse. My flight is checking in."

"Have a safe trip … and don't forget to blow me a kiss from the plane, I will be watching."

Harry smiled and said, "I will message you when I get home."

Clarisse was being brave and did not cry outright. She wanted to show him strength and faith, and not cry like an emotional child. Harry kissed her on the cheek, picked up his bags and started walking to the flight check-in queue. He stopped temporarily, waved at her and smiled. He knew he was coming back, no matter what, and he believed she would be waiting for him. Clarisse blew kisses at him as she waved goodbye. He disappeared past the checkpoint into the main hall of the airport and out of sight.

She felt her phone vibrate several times. It was Harry; he had sent her three emojis of faces blowing a kiss with a winking eye and small flying heart.

She stood there, oblivious to the world around her, and shed a tear.

He will be back—I know he will, she thought.

THE END

HARRY'S NOTE TO CLARISSE

Dear Clarisse,

Our time together has been extraordinary, and I have never felt like this before.

I wanted to tell you about my love plus nothing. It's the type of love that doesn't need to check boxes, or to test each other, or ask our friends what they think. It's a love you should not overthink.

It's about love and nothing else. It just happens, and everyone knows it's right, instinctively. That is what I have found in you: my love plus nothing.

I will see you in three months.

Love, Harry

PS: I hope you like the gold bracelet with the small gold cross!

ABOUT THE AUTHOR

Janice is an Australian author and lives with her family in Melbourne. Janice grew up in South-East Asia and is very well versed in her cultural superstitions and how they influence daily life and customs. She has developed a passion and style for writing paranormal and supernatural novels for new adult readers. The concept of writing the Haunting Clarisse series was spawned over a cup of coffee many years ago. Her books contain heart-thumping, bone-chilling and thought rendering ghost and paranormal experiences that deliver a new twist to every tale.

THE NEXT INSTALMENT

Haunting Clarisse is a three-part series that takes you on a heart-thumping, bone chilling and thought rendering paranormal and supernatural experience that delivers a new twist to every tale.

Janice Tremayne is working on the next book in the series. *Haunting in Hartley*, will become available in May 2020.

To keep up to date with her next book, go to Janice's website.

www.janicetremayne.com

213